CHICKEN OF THOR

RECIPE FOR REVENGE

Praise for
THUNDERCLUCK!

"This absurd premise delivers on its goofy humor ... for those readers not yet ready for Percy Jackson."
—*Bulletin of the Center for Children's Books*

"This rousing adventure introduces a new hero to the world ... [An] epic debut." —*Booklist*

"Tillery dishes out bountiful allusions and wordplay both smart and silly ... [along with] chirpy dialogue, rat-a-tat action, and spry illustrations." —*Publishers Weekly*

"For mythology-loving readers who are too young for Rick Riordan." —*School Library Journal*

"An ideal adventure for more reluctant readers ... An absurd story executed with admirable gravity and skill." —*Kirkus Reviews*

THUNDER CLUCK!

CHICKEN OF THOR

RECIPE FOR REVENGE

WRITTEN BY
PAUL TILLERY IV

CO-ILLUSTRATED BY
PAUL TILLERY IV AND MEG WITTWER

ROARING BROOK PRESS
NEW YORK

For every friendship that's weathered a storm

Text copyright © 2019 by Paul Allen Tillery IV
Illustrations copyright © 2019 by Paul Allen Tillery IV and Meg Wittwer
Published by Roaring Brook Press
Roaring Brook Press is a division of Holtzbrinck Publishing Holdings Limited Partnership
120 Broadway, New York, NY 10271
mackids.com

Library of Congress Control Number: 2019932713

ISBN: 978-1-250-15530-6

Our books may be purchased in bulk for promotional, educational, or business use. Please
contact your local bookseller or the Macmillan Corporate and Premium Sales Department at
(800) 221-7945 ext. 5442 or by email at MacmillanSpecialMarkets@macmillan.com.

First edition, 2019
Printed in the United States of America by LSC Communications,
Harrisonburg, Virginia

1 3 5 7 9 10 8 6 4 2

PROLOGUE

In tales of ancient mystery, in legends of the past,

In thunderstorms, in sacred light,

in shadows dark and vast,

When villains had a recipe for ruin and dismay,

A hero found redemption after friendship went astray.

The hero's path was perilous, and chilling to the bone,

And when the path is darkest,

then we mustn't walk alone.

So let us all remember now,

and let the lore be hallowed:

The tale of Thundercluck against . . .

the Midnight Snack of Shadows.

PART I

OF BISCUITS AND BOOKS

CHAPTER 1
CHICKEN BISCUITS

IN THE REALM OF MIDGARD, SVEN AND
Olga sat down for a picnic. The sun was bright, and
the field was green. It was a lovely day.

Then came the ants.

It started with the smell of hot peppers

wafting on the breeze. Next, there was a rumbling sound and a cloud of smoke in the distance. Sven's face went pale. Olga grabbed her picnic basket, waving it at the ants and saying, "Shoo! Shoo!"

But the ants came swarming closer.

No ordinary ants were these—they were the Fire Ants of Jotunheim, a horde of bugs the size of bison. Flames spurted from their mandibles.

Though the weather was clear, suddenly a thunderbolt struck the ground. The ants stopped in their tracks. A winged girl and a golden chicken dropped from the sky, landing in front of Olga and Sven.

"Thundercluck! Brunhilde!" Sven exclaimed. "Thank the gods you're here!"

The Valkyrie Brunhilde gave him a wink, then lowered her helmet's visor.

The mighty chicken Thundercluck stepped forward. He spread his wings and addressed the ants. "Bagah! Buk-buk-buk." *If you leave in peace, we'll have no quarrel*, he thought. *But if you attack my friends, you might leave in pieces!*

The biggest ant twitched its antennae and pumped its neck. It shot a fireball straight at Thundercluck. He ducked behind his wing as the fire swept over him. It left him singed, but not burned.

It'll take more than that to cook this chicken, he thought, leaping in to attack.

Brunhilde followed suit. Lightning crackled from the chicken's wings, and beams of light blasted from

the Valkyrie's blade. The ants staggered back. They launched more fireballs, but Brunhilde blocked them with her glowing shield.

The leading ant made a chattering sound, and the swarm retreated. They fled the field and were gone.

Elsewhere, a large man-pig wandered through a dark forest. He carried a sack, and every few steps he paused to look under leaves. With each check, he said, "Nope, nuthin' there neither, Mr. Boss."

He stopped at the base of a gnarly tree and scratched his back against it. A silky voice above him called, "You there!"

The man-pig jumped and looked up. A horned owl perched on a branch with her head completely sideways. "Tell me your name," she said. Then she batted her eyelids and added, "I mean, hoo, who are you?"

The man-pig gave a little wave and said, "Muh name's War-Tog."

"And what are you doing in my forest, War-Tog?" asked the owl.

War-Tog shifted his eyes and said, "Lookin' . . . for stuff."

"I see," said the owl, and she squinted at the sack he carried. "What's in that bag?"

War-Tog looked nervous and said, "I'm not s'posed to tell nobody."

"Oh, but you can trust me," said the owl. "We're both talking animals!"

War-Tog scratched his head and said, "That makes sense."

An angry voice from inside the sack said, "No, it doesn't! Don't you dare pull me out, you swine!"

The owl swooped down and ripped the sack with her talons. A big, round object tumbled out, but War-Tog caught it. It was a skull. A skull with a mustache. And a chef's hat.

The owl fluttered toward War-Tog and the skull.

With a puff of black smoke, she transformed into a woman in a crimson cloak.

From War-Tog's hairy hands, the skull frowned and said, "Medda. You shape-shifting show-off. I should've known it was you."

"Gorman Bones," she replied. "Have you forgotten our deal?"

Back at the picnic site, Thundercluck and Brunhilde sat down with Olga and Sven.

"Bless you both," Olga said. "Please, have some biscuits with us!"

Thundercluck had worked up an appetite, and he happily dug in.

"These were made with love," Sven said. "And also butter. It's a magic recipe, and they'll always stay fresh!"

"This is nice," Brunhilde said, "but we'd better get back to Asgard. Heimdall told us not to stay out too long."

Thundercluck stared wistfully at his half-eaten biscuit.

"Please, take these with you," Olga said. She wrapped some biscuits in a cloth and tucked them into Thundercluck's backpack. She patted his head and said, "You're a good chicken."

Sven nodded and said, "Say hi to your mother for me!"

"All right, warrior bird," Brunhilde said. "Want to learn how to use the Bifrost? To get back to Asgard, raise your wing and think about home."

Thundercluck did so, and a rainbow beam carried the heroes away.

Back in the forest, Gorman's skull stammered, "Well, er, about our deal. Of course I didn't *forget*. I've just been busy, that's all."

"So I've heard," Medda replied. "I know all about your little plot—except for War-Tog here, your army fled, spreading the story of your failure far and wide." She leaned closer to Gorman's skull and added, "If it's

any comfort, they seem happier without you."

"Aw, gee," War-Tog said. "That's nice to hear, huh, Mr. Boss? Boss?"

Gorman scowled.

Medda patted

War-Tog's head, her fingernails as sharp as claws. "Such a loyal pig. Such a simple mind." She smirked at Gorman. "Since our conditions have changed, I propose a new deal."

"What do you want?" Gorman asked.

"Something's gone missing in Asgard," Medda said. In an icy voice, she whispered, "The Asgardians shall seek it, but I'll make it my own . . . and then I'll make them suffer."

CHAPTER 2
THE MISSING BOOK

THE HEROES RETURNED TO THE HOLY realm of Asgard. As they stepped down from the Bifrost, a friendly voice called, "Well met, feathered friends!"

It was Heimdall, the watchman of the gods. He had sent them to save the picnic. With his magic sight, he could peer across any distance and into any realm.

"Hi," Brunhilde said. "Everything here still safe?"

Mere weeks had passed since Thundercluck and Brunhilde had defeated Gorman Bones, saving the

realms from certain doom. Asgard still rejoiced. Each new day the heroes reveled in fanfare, festivities, and free dessert at most restaurants.

"All's well," Heimdall answered, "but you've both been summoned to Valhalla's gymnasium. The gods want you to start advanced battle training. They're calling it... the Gym Class of Eternal Struggle."

"Always something, huh?" Brunhilde said. She patted Thundercluck's shoulder.

A chicken's work is never done, he thought. Aloud he said, "Bagock."

The gymnasium was empty when the heroes arrived. Then a gust of wind blew over their wings, and a voice called out, "Greetings, girl and golden bird!"

They turned and saw Freya, the Goddess of Love and War. Brunhilde bowed, and Thundercluck followed suit.

Brunhilde whispered, "Freya's the leader of the Valkyries," and Thundercluck bowed lower still.

"Arise," Freya commanded. "Brunhilde, you have studied well in my Battle Academy. Thundercluck, Thor tells

me you've had some practice, but you lack formal training. Is this true?"

Thundercluck looked at his wings and said, "Bagurk."

"He's largely self-taught," Brunhilde added.

"Then we begin at once!" Freya declared. "Take nine
paces apart, and prepare for combat." The heroes nodded at each other and braced for action, wondering
what foe Freya might throw at them.

"Good," Freya said. "Now that you are ready for
battle . . . face each other."

"Buk-buk?" Thundercluck said. Brunhilde caught
his eye and shrugged.

"Your first lesson is magic defense," Freya said.
"Brunhilde, raise your shield, but do not use your
magic. Thundercluck . . . zap Brunhilde."

Thundercluck looked from the goddess to the
Valkyrie. His eyebrows went up in concern.

"It's all right," Brunhilde said. "Just do a light zap.
I'll be fine."

He pointed his wings at Brunhilde and cast a tiny
bolt. She held fast as the shock traveled through her

shield. A shiver went up her spine, and her wings twitched.

"Whew!" she said. "That'll wake you up in the morning. My elbows feel tingly."

"Again," Freya said, "but this time, Brunhilde, focus your magic into your shield."

Brunhilde concentrated, and her shield began to glow. Thundercluck zapped it again, and this time the lightning bounced away with a BONGGG!

"Well done," Freya said. "Now, Thundercluck, it is your turn to defend."

The chicken gulped.

"Brunhilde, prepare to attack," the goddess commanded, "and Thundercluck, raise your wing in defense."

Thundercluck crouched, guarding with his wing.

"Remember the fireball that hit your wing?" Freya asked. "Your feathers offered some defense, but still the attack left you toasted. You must learn to defend with magic. Use your wits, not just your wings."

Thundercluck tilted his head.

"Feel the lightning flowing within you," Freya said, "and focus it like a shield."

As he did, he felt a charge flow through his wing.

Freya nodded. "Now, Brunhilde. Strike."

Brunhilde's sword cut the air, and an arc of light shot out. The beam deflected off Thundercluck's wing.

"Fine work, young heroes," Freya said, "but I see you were both holding back. I wonder: in a true fight between you two, who would prevail? Shall we try a sparring match?"

Thundercluck let out a nervous "Bwaaak?"

Brunhilde shuffled her feet. She had sparred in her training before, but never with such a close friend.

"Ca-caw! Ca-caw!" a pair of ravens called through the air. They flew to the heroes with scrolls in their talons.

"Huginn! Muninn!" Freya said. "They must bear tidings from Odin— read the scrolls at once."

Brunhilde accepted her scroll with a grin. "If it's a thank-you card from the king," she said, "do we file that under 'Fan Mail' or 'Government Documents'?" But as she opened the scroll, the smile left her face.

Thundercluck looked at his own scroll. It was an overdue notice from the library of Asgard. The chicken remembered visiting the library with Brunhilde. They had found an enchanted book.

"The journal—it was *Magic and Stones May Carry Me Home: The Travels of S. Valkamor*," Brunhilde said. "Everyone was asleep when we took it, but the library's magic must have noticed the checkout."

Thundercluck nodded. The book had been heavily enchanted.

"I forgot all about it," Brunhilde said. "But no problem! I kept it in my Battle Bag, so it should be right here." She peered in her bag, then frantically patted the inside. "I don't understand," she said. "It's gone."

Thundercluck looked at the scroll again. The bottom lines read:

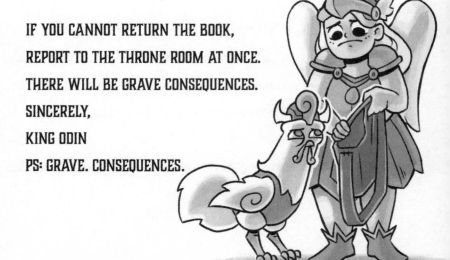

IF YOU CANNOT RETURN THE BOOK,
REPORT TO THE THRONE ROOM AT ONCE.
THERE WILL BE GRAVE CONSEQUENCES.
SINCERELY,
KING ODIN
PS: GRAVE. CONSEQUENCES.

CHAPTER 3
ODIN'S DECREE

THUNDERCLUCK AND BRUNHILDE MADE
their way to the Throne Room. "You've been in Asgard about a year," Brunhilde said. "I was raised here—have you noticed how Odin can be a little particular?"

Thundercluck said nothing.

"Once the royal barber accidentally snipped off half his mustache. As punishment, Odin had a wizard transform the barber into a walrus. And the walrus only had one tusk."

The heroes entered the chamber where King Odin

and Queen Frigg awaited. Thor followed carrying Thundercluck's mother, an Asgardian chicken named Hennda.

Brunhilde leaned to Thundercluck and whispered, "You know you're in trouble when the authorities call your mom." She paused and added, "But at least you know who your mom is."

Odin raised his spear and called, "Bird and Battle Maiden!" His gray beard quivered. "The Valkamor book is long past due, and you two have been slow to answer your summons. What reason have you for this late arrival?"

Brunhilde's eyebrows went up. "Well, we just got back from—"

"What," Odin interrupted, "prancing through Midgard and eating biscuits? Yes, Heimdall has told me of your frolicking."

"I was going to say helping friends," Brunhilde said quietly.

Are we really in trouble? Thundercluck thought. *At least the biscuits were worth it.* He looked at Frigg. Her expression was flat, but Thundercluck caught her rolling her eyes when Odin spoke again.

"Young warriors, you have courage, but you lack obedience," he said. "In this kingdom we follow the rule of law, and we'll not have a missing library book."

The chamber was quiet. Then Brunhilde said, "All right, we won't have it. Technically, we *already* don't have it."

Thundercluck held back a chicken giggle. He was nervous, and that made it hard not to laugh.

"Do you find this funny?" Odin snapped. "Guards! Bring in Madame Runa."

The chamber doors opened for the head librarian from the Asgardian Hall of Books. A pair of spectacles gleamed over her eyes. She bowed and said, "You summoned me, All-father?"

"Madame Runa!" Odin said. "Tell these two the gravity of their offense."

"Well, certainly I want the book returned," she said. "At the same time, I'm just glad to see kids interested in reading—"

"Ahem!" Odin said. "When was the book due back?"

"Two weeks after checkout, Your Highness," said Madame Runa. "That's already passed."

"And for how long," Odin asked, "do you grant the Sacred Grace Period?"

"One lunar phase," Madame Runa replied. "That ends the day after tomorrow."

Odin gazed at Thundercluck and Brunhilde. "There you have it. You have today and tomorrow to search, and you must return the book on the third and final day. In the meantime, I cast a late penalty!" He tapped his spear on the ground, and a bracelet appeared on Brunhilde's wrist. It was shaped like an openmouthed snake about to bite its own tail.

The penalty is . . . exotic jewelry? Thundercluck thought, but Brunhilde's face was grim.

"Since you were the one took who the book," Odin

told Brunhilde, "you shall face the brunt of consequence. You are forbidden from using your magic until the book is returned."

Thundercluck squawked, "Buk-bu—"

"No 'buks' about it!" Odin said. "From this point onward, Brunhilde, you are on a Power Probation!"

Under her breath, Brunhilde said, "And you're on a power *trip*." Then she proclaimed, "Fine. The book must be somewhere in Asgard, so we'll find it. How hard could it be?"

"So you want to steal the book," Gorman said to Medda. His skull leaned sideways in War-Tog's hands. "Why should I care?"

"Oh, no reason," Medda said, "as long as you're happy without a body for the rest of your undead existence."

Gorman narrowed his eye sockets.

"Not so happy, I take it?" Medda smirked. "Yes,

I heard that when your little castle fell, your bones were scattered all across the realms. You must be trying to find them. How's that going?"

War-Tog proudly said, "I found Boss's skull in what wuz left of the kitchen. And I coulda *swore* I found a scapula . . ." He trailed off, then added quietly, "Turns out it was a spatula, and now I know that's sumthin' different."

Gorman sighed.

Medda flashed a sinister grin. "Well, I was going to offer my help, but I see you don't need me. I'll just be going now."

"Wait!" Gorman cried. "War-Tog means well, but his efforts are a bit . . . ham-fisted."

War-Tog thought a moment, then said, "Hey now, that wuzzen—"

"What do you have in mind?" Gorman asked Medda.

"I have a plan," she said, "but it requires your help. You want your bones. I want the book."

"And I'd like a mud bath," War-Tog said.

Gorman cleared his throat. He squinted at Medda and asked, "Why do you want the book so badly?"

"We both want revenge," Medda said. "You tried to get yours, and you failed. If I get that book, not only will I help you find your bones, but all the realms will suffer . . . and I'll show you the meaning of vengeance."

After a silence, War-Tog asked, "Can I have a mud bath after?"

Back in the Throne Room, Brunhilde looked at the snake bracelet on her wrist. "I'm sure we'll find the book on time," she said. "But in case we don't, what happens?"

Odin sternly said, "You shall be banished from Asgard. Forever."

Thundercluck's beak fell open. Brunhilde said, "Whoa, what?"

"And remember, Brunhilde," Odin continued, "you are forbidden from using your magic before the book's return. If you break this rule, that bracelet will sense it. The snake will bite its tail, and your banishment will be immediate."

Thundercluck glared at Odin. *That's absurd*, thought the bird.

"Just to be clear," Brunhilde said, "everyone remembers we saved the universe a few weeks ago, right?"

Queen Frigg opened her mouth to speak, but Odin declared, "The past matters not for the task at hand. Asgardian law is very particular about its library collection."

Turning to Madame Runa, Brunhilde asked, "Has a book ever gone missing before?"

"Once," Madame Runa replied. "And *only* once."

Thundercluck was indignant. He was about to squawk, but the chamber doors flew open and a hush

fell in the Throne Room. In walked Saga, Goddess of Vision and Foresight. As she strode, she spoke:

> My friend, you send these heroes on a quest
> to find the book;
> You order them to seek it, but you know not
> where to look.
> Unless I guide them, I foretell this task will overwhelm.
> By magic most mysterious, the book has left this realm.

Thundercluck's stomach dropped. *Saga's visions are always true,* he thought. *If the book's not in Asgard . . . where could it be?*

CHAPTER 4
THE WYRM

"SAGA," ODIN SAID, "YOUR VISIONS ARE valued, but you cannot just—"

Saga raised a hand, and Odin fell silent. The goddess spoke again:

> *The book must be recovered soon. On that we've all agreed.*
> *But know the quest to take it back is perilous indeed.*
> *Against an ancient mystery, our heroes must stand firm.*
> *I fear the book has fallen to the clutches of the Wyrm.*

Everyone but Thundercluck gasped. *What's the big deal?* he wondered. *I eat worms for breakfast.*

Madame Runa saw Thundercluck's confusion. "This is no ordinary creature," she whispered. "We librarians speak of it in hushed tones . . . the Book Wyrm, mystic collector of missing tomes. Its location is a mystery."

"Yeah," Brunhilde said. "I learned about Wyrms—spelled with a 'y'—in Valhalla's academy. They're super-rare serpents with near-invincible scales, razor-sharp tails, and acid spit."

"The Book Wyrm is all those things," Madame Runa said, "and a ferocious reader."

"So, Odin," Brunhilde said, "this changes things, right? The Book Wyrm's dangerous, and we don't even know where it is, so . . . can we have a deadline extension?"

"No," Odin said. "Once I've declared it, my rule is law."

Queen Frigg had been silent, but she cleared her throat. She put her hand on Odin's shoulder and said,

"Darling, reconsider. You started making rules before you knew all the facts." Thor nodded, and Hennda cooed in his hands. Frigg leaned to Odin's ear and whispered, "If you feel guilty about the Gorman incident, this isn't the way to—"

"Do you see this eye patch?" Odin said, pointing to his face. Eons ago, he had traded one of his eyes to a magical being. "I gave my eye so that I would be wise, and I will not be questioned!"

"Okay," Brunhilde said, "but if we could just—"

"My declarations are final," Odin said. "Such it is to be king."

"Then as queen," Frigg said, "if I can't change your rule, I'll add to it." She turned to the heroes. "The goddess Freya will join you on this quest! And Heimdall will be watching you." She glanced back at Odin and added, "At least some of the adults here wish to keep our children safe."

That's a relief, Thundercluck thought, but Brunhilde seemed irritated.

"And one last rule," Odin said. "Given your recent

playtime in Midgard, you are not to use the Bifrost again until you have the book. Otherwise..."

"We'll be banished?" Brunhilde guessed flatly.

"...you'll be banished." Odin nodded.

"Anything else?" Brunhilde asked. "We need to pack. Do I get banished if I forget my toothbrush?"

Thundercluck saw Queen Frigg hide a smile.

"One doesn't find books with sass," Odin replied. "Now go, for the glory of Asgard!"

The heroes rode out in Freya's chariot, drawn by her two cats, Bygul and Trygul. The cats pulled the chariot across the Asgardian plains.

Thundercluck's stomach grumbled, and he peeked in his bag for a snack. He decided to save Olga's biscuits for breakfast the next morning. In the meantime he had birdseed, his other favorite snack.

"So, Freya," Brunhilde said. "About our new battle classes. Does this count as a field trip? Maybe extra credit?"

Freya's eyes looked serious, but a hint of a smile crossed her face. "Every challenge is an opportunity to learn, and you're a terrific student. But let us not forget: you're technically still in trouble."

"Right," Brunhilde said. "We have to find the book. What do you know about it?"

"It contains powerful knowledge," Freya replied. "In the wrong hands, it could be dangerous."

"It was written by someone named S. Valkamor," Brunhilde said. "Any idea who that is?"

Freya looked into the distance and said, "Odin commanded long ago we not talk about Valkamor."

"Odin commands a lot of stuff, huh?" said Brunhilde. Freya didn't reply, so Brunhilde changed the subject. "Where are we looking first? We can't take the Bifrost, so probably not Midgard, right?"

The chariot slowed. Bygul had paused to roll on his back, and Trygul was licking his paws. Freya jiggled the reins, and the cats started moving again. "I'd like to start with a theory," Freya said. "We can find worms in a garden, can we not? Then perhaps we'll find a magic Wyrm in a magic garden. And which realm might that be?"

Thundercluck remembered a realm they had visited before, vibrant with plants and flowers. Brunhilde said, "Alfheim, but how—"

Freya held up a key she wore on a necklace. She closed her eyes, silently mouthed an incantation, and turned the key in midair. Rainbow light swirled in an arch before the chariot. Thundercluck peered into the arch and saw a garden landscape. It was like looking through an open door. The cats pulled the chariot through the arch, and it closed behind them. They were in Alfheim.

"Wow!" Brunhilde said. "How did you do that? Thundercluck and I had so much trouble going through the realms!"

"This is a Spectrum Key," Freya said wearily, her hand still on the necklace. "Queen Frigg lent it from her royal key chain. Very few of these relics exist, and they require great energy to—Bygul, Trygul, no! Bad cats!"

Bygul and Trygul had wriggled out of their harnesses and were running through the garden. Bygul chewed on leaves. Trygul squatted in a potted plant.

"Stop that at once!" Freya said.

The cats continued.

Brunhilde found a pouch of Asgardian cat treats on the chariot's floor. She shook the pouch, and the cats came running. They rubbed against her shins. With a nod from Freya, Brunhilde fed them treats. Thundercluck stroked Trygul with his wing, and he purred.

Freya put the cats back in their harnesses. She squinted at the plants and the setting sun. "We should make camp," she said, "and then we'll consider the Wyrm. Stay on guard; these plants have minds of their own, and they might seek revenge for the cats' indignities."

"If you say so," Brunhilde replied, "but last time Thundercluck and I were here, it seemed perfectly safe."

Thundercluck thought he saw a vine move. He turned for a closer look, but all was still. *Stay on guard indeed*, he thought, and he whispered, "Bagahhh."

They made camp at the edge of a forest. Night had fallen.

Freya ran her hands over a tree's bark. "Alfheim's plants serve well for alchemy," she said. "Tonight we'll make a Seeker's Potion, and tomorrow we'll look for the Wyrm. For the potion, we'll need Seeds of Doubt, Fruits of Labor, and Quest Nuts. I shall gather them now."

Brunhilde perked up and asked, "Can we come?"

"No," Freya replied. "The woods are dark and twisted, and I don't want you wandering off. Watch the cats, and again, stay on guard."

Thundercluck and Brunhilde sat together, petting the cats. "What a day, huh?" said Brunhilde. She looked at the bracelet on her wrist. "I miss my magic already."

"Buk-buk," Thundercluck said. *It's not fair*, he thought, *but we should just find the book and be done with it.*

"And why do you think Odin won't let Freya talk about Valkamor?" Brunhilde said. "If the book was Valkamor's journal, he must have traveled a lot. Just like us! I almost feel like—what's that noise?"

They heard a rustling nearby, and a horde of thorny vines came snaking from the forest. The cats leapt into the chariot, hissing with their tails puffed out. Thundercluck and Brunhilde jumped to their feet.

Brunhilde drew her sword and shield. "I hope you've got your magic ready," she said, "'cause I can't use mine."

Thundercluck gulped. The cats hissed.

The vines crept closer.

CHAPTER 5
ON THE LAMB

THUNDERCLUCK GLANCED AT BRUNHIL-de's bracelet. On their last journey, the bird had lost his powers and Brunhilde had protected him. *How the tables have turned*, he thought. He glared at the vines, thinking, *WHO WANTS SOME CHICKEN?*

He launched a bolt at the approaching vines. Kra-KOWW! Thunder shook the air. The vines shriveled and fell to the ground. A smell like burned broccoli filled the air.

More vines crept forward.

"Ba-GERRK!" cried Thundercluck, unleashing another

bolt. He swept his wing sideways, and lightning fried more of the wiggly weeds.

The cats had hidden inside the chariot, and a single vine slithered their way. Brunhilde chopped it with her sword. It lay still.

Brunhilde scanned their surroundings. "I think that's it," she said. "Nice job, buddy!"

Thundercluck puffed out his chest, but the forest rustled again. From inside the chariot, one of the cats let out an anxious "reeooowwwwww."

A bigger surge of vines emerged, and the heroes returned to battle stance. Thundercluck's eyes went

wide. He started launching bolts faster than before. The vines sizzled, but with each bolt Thundercluck felt weaker. He needed time to recharge.

Brunhilde slashed another vine as it reached for the cats. She noticed Thundercluck's fatigue and thought about her own magic. She wondered if she would still get banished if she used it to save others. "I'm not going to let my friend get hurt," she muttered. "Time to slice some vegetables." She gripped her sword and prepared her powers.

Just then, a gust of wind blew in. Freya descended from the sky, radiant wings open wide. She slashed her glistening sword, shooting forth another blast of wind. The remaining vines shrank back into the woods.

All was quiet except the sizzling vines and the growling cats. Bygul and Trygul emerged from the chariot, hair still standing on end.

The goddess poked a leaf on a fallen vine. "The Poison Ivy of Alfheim," she said. "Its lightest touch can itch for ages, and extreme exposure is deadly. You did well to hold it off." She patted Thundercluck. "With practice, your thunder will grow ever stronger. And Brunhilde, I know you were tempted, but I am glad you withheld your power."

"Yeah," Brunhilde muttered. "Otherwise I might've helped my friend."

"We should focus on the task at hand," Freya said. "For the Seeker's Potion, I gathered the seeds and fruits we need, but there were no Quest Nuts to be found. It was as if someone had already plucked them all. The nuts only grow at dawn, so we'll have to make the potion tomorrow. For now, let's rest."

Thundercluck slept soundly, but Brunhilde woke him in the night. "Hey, buddy," she said, her head poking into his tent. "I was on guard duty, and I heard a noise." They listened for a moment and heard a distant "ba-a-a."

"There it is again!" Brunhilde said. "Want to check it out with me?"

The chicken rubbed his eyes and said a sleepy "Bagurrk."

Thundercluck stepped out and looked at Freya's tent. The goddess snoozed within.

"We should let her sleep," Brunhilde said. "You saw how tired she was after using that magic key, and then she attacked those vines. Even the gods need rest!"

The heroes listened as another "ba-a-a" came from the forest. They started toward the noise, creeping into the pitch-black woods. "Sure would be nice to light up my sword," Brunhilde said.

Thundercluck thought for a moment and focused his magic into a glowing spark. It hovered before them, casting a pale blue light. He squinted proudly and thought, *I fixed the problem!* But Brunhilde was still frowning. *Maybe that wasn't the real problem,* Thundercluck realized.

"Odin and Frigg treat me like a baby," Brunhilde muttered. "But they're not my parents. They won't even tell me who my parents are!"

They heard the "ba-a-a" sound again, this time much closer. They came upon a clearing, bright with moonlight, and at its center sat a little lamb.

"It's so cute!" Brunhilde said.

"Greetings!" said the lamb in a silky voice.

"And it can TALK!" Brunhilde exclaimed.

Thundercluck felt a pang of jealousy. He let his spark go out.

"I've been sent by Asgard," said the lamb, "with a message about your quest. You are to continue without Freya, and to find the book, you should seek the author."

"Valkamor?" Brunhilde said. "We can find out who Valkamor is?"

That doesn't sound like the plan, Thundercluck thought.

"That's the plan!" said the lamb. Brunhilde looked excited, but Thundercluck nudged her and cocked an eyebrow.

"So you're from Asgard, too?" Brunhilde asked. "What's your official title?"

"Uh . . . Lambassador," said the lamb. "You can trust me—I'm a talking animal!"

Brunhilde put her hand on her chin and said, "Well, your horns are awful cute . . ."

The lamb leaned closer and said, "Better yet, I can tell you how to find Valkamor."

That was all Brunhilde needed to hear. "We'll do it!" she said. "How do we start?"

Thundercluck shifted on his feet, uncertain.

"No time to hesitate," said the lamb. "The path ahead is dangerous, so you'll need to recite a spell to avoid being watched."

"I can do that," Brunhilde said, "but what about Thundercluck? He can't speak."

Thundercluck stiffened and said a brusque "B'gah."

"Aww, he thinks he's a person," the lamb said. Thundercluck glared at her. "Just recite the spell with your hand on his wing," the lamb told Brunhilde.

Brunhilde grabbed Thundercluck's wing. He tried to pull away, but she held on. He relaxed his wing and scowled.

"I can see you're both excited!" said the lamb. "Now repeat after me." She said the following words, and Brunhilde repeated:

I cast myself upon this night
Away from Asgard, out of sight!

Back in Asgard, Heimdall woke with a start. He climbed his watchtower to check on the heroes. He had followed their journey into Alfheim and watched Freya defeat the vines. Now he found Freya once more... but Thundercluck and Brunhilde were nowhere to be seen.

Eyes wide, he asked, "What trickery is this?"

"That did the trick!" said the lamb with a smile. "Now, about your quest: to find Valkamor, first you'll need to meet the dwarves. What do you know of them?"

"I know they're master craftspeople," Brunhilde said, "and they don't always get along with Asgard." She thought about Odin's style of ruling, and added dryly, "I wonder why. I also know they like to dig tunnels, and they live in the realm of Nidavellir." She paused. "And without the magic guide book, we can't find our way there."

Well, thunder-shucks, thought Thundercluck. *I guess we'll have to go back to Freya.*

"Not so fast," the lamb replied. "It's true that Nidavellir's their home world, but there's a trio of Dwarven Travelers exploring elsewhere. They craft transportation relics and build magic tunnels to connect the realms."

"That's great," Brunhilde said, "but we still have no way to find them."

"Not with *that* attitude," said the lamb. "You carry that fancy sword around, but you don't know half of what it can do!"

Thundercluck perked up, intrigued.

"There's an inscription on the hilt that's only visible in moonlight," said the lamb. "Take a look and read what it says."

Brunhilde raised her sword into a moonbeam. She had polished the hilt a dozen times, but now it showed words she had never seen before. Out loud, she read:

From hand, to wrist, to elbow joint,
Seek out the dwarves, and stay on point!

The sword almost flew away, but she held it in her grip. "This is new," she said. It pulled strongly in her hand, pointing deeper into the forest.

Pointing farther away from Freya, Thundercluck noticed.

"The sword will pull you on a path to the Dwarven Travelers," explained the lamb. "The pulling will stop anytime you reach a dwarven site, or if you need the sword for combat. When you're ready to get back on the search, just say the spell again!"

Thundercluck gave the lamb a dirty look and pecked Brunhilde's bracelet.

"Oh, right," she said. "I'm not supposed to use magic."

"Did Odin say no magic *at all*," asked the lamb, "or did he say not to use *your* magic? Because technically, this is the sword's magic, not yours." Her snout curled in a grin. "Don't you just love loopholes?"

"Works for me," Brunhilde said. "Come on, Thundercluck! To glory ... and to Valkamor!" She marched into the woods without looking back.

I feel like I haven't been heard, Thundercluck thought, but still he followed.

The lamb watched the heroes go. Once they were out of sight, she said, "All too easy. You can come out now."

War-Tog shuffled into the clearing from behind a tree, munching on a handful of Quest Nuts.

"I didn't pluck those for you to eat," said the lamb. With a poof of black smoke, she transformed into Medda. "We just had to keep them from Freya—I'm not even sure they're edible."

War-Tog shrugged and ate another. From the crook of his arm, Gorman's skull said, "Well played, Medda. I'm impressed."

"You should be." She looked where the heroes had gone. "That went perfectly."

Under the Asgardian night sky, King Odin and Queen Frigg arrived at the watchtower. Odin yawned and asked, "For what have you interrupted our slumber?"

"My king," Heimdall said, "I can still see Freya at her camp, but by some treachery... I've lost sight of the children."

"How could this happen?" Frigg demanded.

A sharp tap rang out behind them. The gods turned to see Saga, who rapped her staff again on the stone floor. She lifted a hand and said:

*By sorcerous deceptions have the
heroes been misled.
Upon a path of darkness now they
both must lightly tread.
Against the challenges to come,
they'll need their wits
and talents;
To find the book, the race is on . . .
and fate hangs
in the balance.*

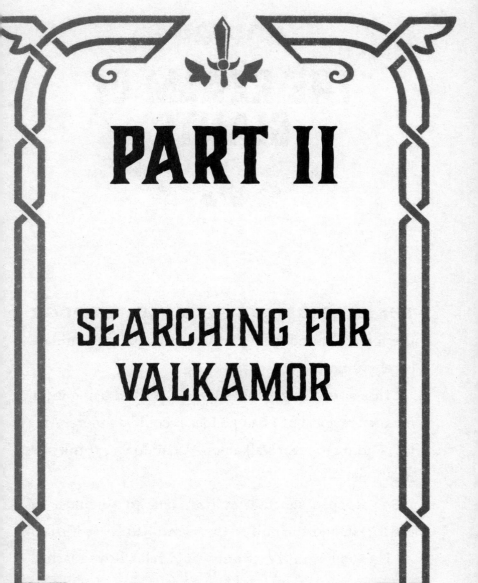

PART II

SEARCHING FOR VALKAMOR

CHAPTER 6
THE REALM OF GIANTS

THE HEROES MADE THEIR WAY THROUGH the forest. Thundercluck lit another spark. Brunhilde barely noticed.

"This sword is so cool," she said. "I liked using it for my own magic, but I had no idea it could do more! And we're going to meet Valkamor! What do you think he's like? I bet—"

She stopped short. They had come to a boulder in the forest, and the pull of the sword had ceased.

"The lamb said the sword would relax if we reached a dwarven site," Brunhilde said. She patted her free

hand on the boulder. "But I don't see any tunnel, just this rock!" She tapped it with the Dwarven Blade, and runes began to glow on the boulder's surface. They revealed a message that read:

A DOOR THAT'S CLOSED CAN BE EXPOSED
BY MAGIC WORDS—THE SPOKEN KIND!
WHEN GATES ARE LOCKED, AND BRAINS ARE BLOCKED,
A HERO NEEDS...

"Looks like a riddle," Brunhilde said. "I guess we need to complete the last line with some kind of magic password." She reread the first three lines and said, "I think it's supposed to rhyme with 'the spoken kind.' A hero needs . . . an axe to grind?"

Nothing happened.

Thundercluck looked closely at the words "closed," "locked," and "brains are blocked." He thought of a phrase that would address all those things and excitedly tapped Brunhilde's arm. Once he had her attention, he placed his wings on his forehead and then spread them wide.

Brunhilde squinted and said, "Magic words, the spoken kind . . . a hero needs . . . an open mind?"

The whole boulder flashed with light, and when it dimmed, a tunnel had opened on its side. Rainbow-colored crystals glowed inside.

"Nice work, buddy!" Brunhilde said. "It's a magic gateway! Let's check it out."

Thundercluck still worried about leaving Freya, but he was proud of solving the puzzle. It felt good to be on an adventure with his friend again. Then he remembered the lamb and thought, *What if there's devilry afoot?* Aloud he said, "Buk-buk-bwaaah . . ."

"Come on," Brunhilde said, patting his back. "We're heroes, remember? We don't need a babysitter." Thundercluck's pride swelled, and he followed her into the tunnel.

As the duo marched out of sight, a horned lizard crept to the magic boulder. In a poof of black smoke, it transformed into Medda. "Hurry up, bonehead," she whispered.

War-Tog tiptoed to join her, careful not to step on twigs. "Were you talkin' to me, or to Mr. Boss?" he asked, holding up Gorman's skull.

"Yes," Medda said. "Now that you're here, don't move—I'll cover our tracks."

Footprints from Thundercluck, Brunhilde, and War-Tog led through the soil to the boulder. War-Tog's tracks were especially large. Medda snapped her fingers, and all the footprints vanished.

"Was that really necessary," Gorman asked, "or are you just showing off?"

"Your carelessness was your undoing," Medda replied. "By the time Freya realizes something's up, this tunnel will be closed. As long as we leave no trace, she'll never know we've been here."

"I still think you're showing off," Gorman said.

"Deal with it," Medda said. "We're going in, but stay back enough that those featherbrains don't see or hear us. Got it?"

Gorman wiggled his skull in a nod.

War-Tog said, "Yes, ma'am."

"Don't call me 'ma'am,'" Medda said.

"Sorry, ma'am," War-Tog replied.

Medda rolled her eyes, and she tiptoed into the tunnel.

Thundercluck and Brunhilde forged ahead in the crystal tunnel. The air became cooler, and moonlight shone ahead. They stepped through another boulder and into a foreign realm.

The heroes had emerged from the side of a mountain. Brunhilde pointed down at a huge footprint in the snow, much longer than Brunhilde was tall.

"We're in Jotunheim," Brunhilde said. "The realm of giants. It's also the home of those ants we fought in Midgard, so we should be careful not to drop any food . . . that's how you get ants."

Thundercluck shivered. It was freezing, and he wanted to go back to sleep. Worry crept into his mind—their first day of searching was spent, and every minute brought the deadline closer.

Brunhilde pointed to a cave on a cliff. "Let's camp there," she said. They flew to the site, and Brunhilde opened her bag.

"Bwak!" Thundercluck squawked. He realized he had left his own bag at Freya's camp—when they were looking for the noise, he thought they would come right back. He looked at Brunhilde's bag and wondered, *Why didn't she?*

Brunhilde caught his eye and quickly looked away. "It's not like I *wanted* to leave Freya," she said. "I just wanted to be ready if we *had* to. Don't worry, I brought enough camping stuff for both of us. I'll share!"

As the heroes settled in on the cliff, Medda emerged from the tunnel. "Come on," she whispered. "We haven't got all night!"

War-Tog stumbled through the boulder's opening,

bent low and holding Gorman's skull. "I liked those crystals," he said, "but I coulda used more headroom."

"The dwarves dug it for themselves," Medda said, "not for a big, bumbling pig."

War-Tog frowned and lowered his ears.

Medda shifted to her horned owl form. "I've got spying to do," she said. "You two stay out of sight." She turned away and spread her wings.

"Hold it," Gorman said. The owl's body stayed still, but its head rotated back to stare at him. "Why should you have all the fun?" he asked. "If we're partners, I want to spy, too."

"Fine," Medda said, and she returned to her normal form. "I'm not going to carry you—that's more of a pig job—but you can use this." She pulled a long spyglass from her sleeve.

"Your arms have secrets, too?" War-Tog asked. "So do mine. One time, I found a potato chip in my armpit." Gorman and Medda were silent. "It was salty," War-Tog added.

Medda cleared her throat. "The spyglass is magic.

When you use it to watch someone, it lets you hear them, too."

"Ooh," War-Tog said. "Does it have a name?"

Medda rolled her eyes and said, "I'm only concerned with using my tools, not naming them."

"I'm gonna call it the Nosy-Scope," War-Tog said.

Medda gave him a flat look, but before she could respond, Gorman said, "That'll do, pig." Then he squinted and asked, "If you're so well prepared, Medda, why do you need me?"

"The Wyrm has the book," Medda said. "I know where it is, but the only way there is through Valkamor. My plan requires a recipe that only you can cook." She paused, then added in a whisper, "The Midnight Snack of Shadows."

War-Tog shivered.

"How deliciously sinister!" Gorman said. "The book must be well hidden indeed. How do you know where it is, when even the Asgardians don't?"

"I make it my business to know secrets," Medda said. "Even Heimdall has blind spots, but if you stay low and use the right trinkets"—she handed the spy-glass to War-Tog—"there's no limit to what you can see." She transformed back to her owl form and took off into the night.

Thundercluck awoke in the morning, excited to finally eat his biscuits. But his stomach dropped as he remembered: the biscuits were still in his bag, which he had left behind with Freya. He shouted a grumpy "Ba-gawwk!"

"Did you forget your food, buddy?" Brunhilde asked.

Hmph, thought Thundercluck. *Does it count as "forgetting" if you didn't tell me we should pack?*

"It's okay," Brunhilde said. "I have some extra food in my Battle Bag's magic snack pouch." She split a bagel in two. They each ate half, and Thundercluck still felt hungry. He peered at Brunhilde's bag.

"All I have now is a loaf of sourdough bread," she said. "Here, try a bite."

Thundercluck tried it. He spit it out.

"Well, I'm sorry it's no biscuit," Brunhilde said, "but it's a special Asgardian recipe with all the nutrition we need."

Thundercluck looked at the bread on the ground and thought, *But it's yucky.*

Brunhilde ate a piece with a smile and said, "Let me know if you change your mind."

On a distant cliff, War-Tog held the Nosy-Scope to Gorman's eye socket.

"Hold it steady, you swine!" Gorman barked.

"I'm doin' my best, Mr. Boss," War-Tog replied. "And like you always say, you're proud of me no matter what."

"I never say that," Gorman muttered.

"I still know," War-Tog said, patting Gorman's skull.

Medda flew back as an owl and resumed her normal form. She looked toward the heroes and asked Gorman, "Did you catch all that?"

"Not all of it," Gorman said, glaring at War-Tog, "but enough. The Midnight Snack of Shadows is a most interesting request. Its recipe varies depending on whom it's for."

"Spare me the details," Medda said. "Just tell me: can you do what we've discussed?"

"It's possible," Gorman said, "but it won't be easy. Regarding our bargain, what if just finding my bones isn't payment enough?"

"Then I'll sweeten the deal," Medda replied. "I know you tried to eat Thundercluck before. If you help me with this plan, when all is said and done, that chicken will be yours to devour."

Gorman's mustache curled in a grin. "Now we're cooking."

CHAPTER 7
A SLEEPING GIANT

BRUNHILDE PUT AWAY THE SOURDOUGH and held up her sword. Its inscription had disappeared.

"From arm...wait, no," Brunhilde said. "Ahem. From hand, to wrist, to elbow joint, seek out the dwarves, and stay on point!" The sword began to pull, pointing to the cold wilderness of Jotunheim.

Thundercluck looked back to where the tunnel had been. All he saw was solid rock.

"Come on, buddy!" Brunhilde said. "We don't have time to go back. We've got to find Valkamor!"

Freya returned to the Asgardian Throne Room, distraught. "I couldn't find them anywhere!" she told her fellow gods. "Not even a footprint—all trace of them has vanished!"

"These are dark tidings indeed," Frigg said. "Odin, you've been too stern!"

"Now is no time for finger-pointing!" Odin said.

"Now is the time to take responsibility," Frigg replied.

Odin grumbled, "That's not what being king is about." Then he declared, "Freya! Take Valhalla's finest warriors, and redouble your search in Alfheim! Leave no garden unsearched."

Thor raised his hammer and said, "I will join them, Father!"

"No," Odin said. "We need you here. If treachery is afoot, we must be on guard."

"I implore you," Frigg said, "reverse the spells you've cast on the children. Let Brunhilde use her magic. Let both of them use the Bifrost. Their safety is more important than a library collection."

"If only I could," Odin said. He gazed in the distance as if pondering a cosmic mystery. "Can a god cast a spell so powerful that even he himself cannot break it?" Then he looked at Frigg and said, "Yes. I did. End of story."

Saga cleared her throat, and all the gods turned in attention. She spoke:

Our searching efforts are no match for sinister designs.
We'll try to scan the gardens, yes, but nothing
shall we find.

Beyond our gaze the heroes go! They venture

unprotected . . .

I sense the duo's journey takes them farther than expected.

Thundercluck felt like he had been walking through snow and rocks for hours. Brunhilde had warned that giants were dangerous, so the heroes had to stay low. That meant no flying, and that meant tired chicken legs.

Brunhilde was full of energy, which made Thundercluck even more tired. "I wonder how soon we'll meet Valkamor," she said. "I wonder what he's like! From his journal, we know he's a traveler, and he seems to like poetry and animals. Remember those riddles? They were all animal-themed. Valkamor seems so cool! Just from the journal, I feel like I have a connection to him."

Thundercluck nodded. He was partially listening but more intent on looking for food. *All I've eaten today is half a bagel*, he thought. In any other realm, he would eat a bug or a worm. In this realm, though, the bugs and worms were bigger than he was. He saw an inch-worm that was more like a yard-worm and quickly averted his eyes. His stomach grumbled, and he pecked at Brunhilde's bag.

"Want to try another bite of sourdough?" Brunhilde asked.

Define "want," Thundercluck thought, but he nodded. Brunhilde gave him a piece of bread, and he promptly spit it out.

"Thundercluck, that's the fourth time you've done that," Brunhilde said crossly. "This snack pouch may be bottomless, but I only had one loaf to pack. I'm not sharing any more if you're just going to waste it."

Before Thundercluck could answer, the ground shook under his feet. The heroes had reached a patch of geysers. Steam swirled ahead. Brunhilde's sword pointed into the mist, and a shadowy mass groaned within. After a quiet moment, it swelled and groaned again.

The heroes crept forward. Approaching the mass in the mist, they saw an enormous foot, its toes rising higher than Brunhilde's head. Another foot lay nearby, and both extended from a massive pair of pajama pants. Another groan filled the air, and the shadowy form swelled. It was a snoring, sleeping giant.

"We shouldn't wake him," Brunhilde whispered. A geyser let out a puff of steam, and she added, "I think he's having a spa day."

Thundercluck remembered facing a giantess when he had first come to Asgard. The heroes' magic had faltered when they'd battled the foe directly, so they had tricked it into attacking a dragon.

"No dragon this time," Brunhilde barely breathed as they tiptoed by the sleeping hulk. "So let's—"

She was interrupted by a familiar chatter. Something smelled like hot peppers.

"The Fire Ants of Jotunheim!" Brunhilde whispered.
The duo looked back. Sure enough, they saw dozens of
the same giant ants they had fought in Midgard.

"What did I tell you about dropping food?" Brunhilde hissed.

Thundercluck lowered his head.

A swarm of ants encircled the duo. More were perched
on the surrounding cliffs, ready to pounce if the heroes
tried to fly. The sleeping giant snored, shaking the
ground beneath their feet. More steam spurted from
the geysers.

"Battle stances," Brunhilde whispered. The heroes
would have to fight.

CHAPTER 8
THROUGH THE MUD

ONE OF THE ANTS LAUNCHED A FIREBALL at Brunhilde. Thundercluck remembered his defensive training and blocked it with his wing.

"Thanks, buddy!" Brunhilde whispered. She glanced at the sleeping giant and said, "Strike back, but we've got to keep it quiet!"

Thundercluck shocked the ant with a small bolt. It made a BZZT! sound instead of the usual booming thunder. The ant jolted back, but not by much. It looked angry.

Brunhilde twirled her sword. The ants were still far

enough away they could be hit only with long-range attacks. She felt more tempted than ever to use her magic, but she remembered the bracelet on her wrist.

Thundercluck zapped ant after ant. He could keep these mini zaps going all day without getting tired, but it was barely keeping the bugs at bay. The ants were getting closer.

Three more fireballs hissed through the geyser steam. Thundercluck dug his talons in the ground and flapped his wings, causing a gust of wind. The fireballs blew out like candles, and the ants fell back. *Take that!* the chicken thought, but the ants immediately scuttled to their feet.

The giant stirred in its sleep. "We're pushing our luck, buddy," Brunhilde said. "We need to think of something fast!"

Thundercluck pecked her bag, hoping she would read his mind. He zapped another ant.

Brunhilde opened her bag's snack pouch. The single loaf of bread lay within. If thrown, it would distract the ants for only a moment. They needed something bigger.

Her eyes lit up. She had taken bread on many travels and had never cleaned the bag afterward. The snack pouch was infinite. Thus, it contained nearly infinite crumbs.

"Hey, Thundercluck," she said, "flap your wings at this!" She held open the snack pouch, made sure the rest of the sack's contents were secure, and swung the bag.

A huge cloud of crumbs poured out. It seemed to drift through the air in slow motion. The ants paused to watch it, transfixed.

Thundercluck turned to the crumbs and gave his wings a mighty flap. His eyes went wide as he realized which way he was facing. The crumbs shot through the air . . . and straight up the giant's pajamas.

The giant ants ran into his giant pants.

Brunhilde's eyebrows nearly jumped off her head. The giant woke with a shout and bolted upright. The ground shook as he hopped from foot to foot, wiggling his legs to dance out the ants.

"Time to go!" Brunhilde yelled, darting sideways as a stomp landed next to her. "They're distracted—let's forget the no-flying rule!" As she and Thundercluck flew away, she gave a parting shout of "Sorry! Very sorry!"

Once the heroes had flown far enough to feel safe, they landed and caught their breath. Relief washed over them, and Brunhilde grinned. Thundercluck let out a chicken chuckle, and soon they were laughing together.

This is nice, Thundercluck thought. *Things have been tense, and it's good to laugh with my friend.* He remembered how supportive Brunhilde had always been, and he felt a twinge of guilt for being so grumpy about the bread.

After they finished giggling, Brunhilde raised her sword and repeated the spell. The two followed the blade to a marsh of bubbling mud pits.

They started down a path between the puddles. A deep voice behind them said, "Oh boy, oh boy! Can we stop for a mud bath?"

The heroes whipped around and saw a large man-pig. He seemed to have just realized he was speaking out loud.

Brunhilde gripped her shield and said, "War-Tog. I remember you. What are you doing here?"

War-Tog lowered his snout toward the ground. A horned toad sitting on his foot shook its head. The man-pig looked back up and said, "Uh . . . nuthin'."

"Who were you talking to?" Brunhilde asked.

". . . Also nuthin'."

Thundercluck had a lightning bolt at the ready. Brunhilde raised her sword.

"Wait," War-Tog said, raising his hands. "I don't wanna fight. I didn't wanna fight last time, neither. I was just followin' orders."

Thundercluck looked in the man-pig's eyes. He nodded at Brunhilde and said, "Bagurr."

She lowered her sword and said, "All right. But next time someone tells you to do something, and you know it's wrong, you should think for yourself."

War-Tog scratched his head. "So I shouldn't take orders. Is that . . . is that an order?"

Thundercluck's head spun. *Am I dizzy because that's a paradox*, he wondered, *or because all I've eaten today is half a bagel?* His stomach grumbled again.

Brunhilde thought a moment and said, "I *highly encourage* you to think for yourself, but you don't *have to* listen to me."

"I gotta think about that," War-Tog said. He glanced at the puddles and added, "Maybe over a nice, long mud bath."

"Up to you," Brunhilde said. "We'll be going now." She and Thundercluck turned and pressed on.

Once the heroes were far out of sight, a cloud of black smoke poofed next to War-Tog, and Medda stood where the horned toad had been. She glared at War-Tog, lifting Gorman's skull from behind a rock, where she had hidden him.

Gorman had been trying not to laugh, but in Medda's hands he finally cackled. "Think for yourself!" he exclaimed. "As if War-Tog could ever do that!"

"Let's keep moving," Medda said.

War-Tog drooped his ears and asked, "Whuddabout my mud bath?"

Medda tucked Gorman's skull under her arm and said, "Imbecile." She walked on.

"Guys?" War-Tog called. He took one last look at the mud, then slouched and followed Medda.

With the sword re-enchanted, Thundercluck and Brunhilde marched ahead. "We've seen giant rocks, giant bugs, and giant puddles," Brunhilde said. "Wherever this sword is taking us, there'd better be a giant payoff."

I could use a giant lunch, Thundercluck thought.

They neared the ruins of a tremendous castle. The blade pulled harder in Brunhilde's hand. "Whoa," she

said, digging her heels in the dirt. The sword yanked forward, and Brunhilde broke into a run.

Thundercluck trotted after her. Darting through the ruins, they charged toward a giant mushroom. Underneath it stood three dwarves with helmets, beards, and colorful tunics. The dwarves carried scrolls, and

they were surveying the ruins and adding to maps. They paused to watch the approaching heroes.

The sword came to a rest.

"Uh, hi," Brunhilde said.

"Buk-buk," Thundercluck added. He waved a wing.

"Asgardians," one of the dwarves said to his companions. "Can we trust them?"

"Yes," said another. "Behold: she bears a Dwarven Blade."

"Indeed," said the third. He walked closer to Brunhilde and said, "She must be the daughter of Valkamor."

CHAPTER 9
THE DWARVEN TRAVELERS

THUNDERCLUCK'S BEAK FELL OPEN.

"Valkamor's my dad?" Brunhilde shouted, gobsmacked. The dwarves were silent. "Do you know him?" she asked. "Can we meet him?"

"Let us start with introductions," said the dwarf closest to Brunhilde. His tunic shimmered with the warm colors of candlelight. "I am Roy, leader of the Dwarven Travelers. These are my friends, Gee and Biv." Gee's tunic glistened like an emerald. Biv's reminded Thundercluck of the sky right after a sunset.

"Valkamor," Roy said, "is a great hero to the dwarves.

That sword has been enchanted so only a descendant of Valkamor can wield it."

"And we've been using it to find him!" Brunhilde said.

Has she forgotten the book? Thundercluck thought. *That's how we got into this mess. Also, do dwarves carry snacks?*

Roy held Brunhilde's gaze. "You have many questions," he said.

"As do all curious minds," said Gee.

"Yes," said Biv, looking at Thundercluck. "Like which came first, the chicken or the egg?"

Trick question, thought Thundercluck. *It was the THUNDER!* Unable to speak, he tried to make eye contact with Brunhilde. She tended to know what he was thinking, but now her attention was fully on Roy.

"There is much you don't understand, daughter of Valkamor," the dwarven leader said. "It is not our place to explain, but we can guide you on your path. Did you take one of our tunnels into this realm?"

Brunhilde nodded.

"There is another tunnel not far beyond these ruins," said Roy. "It shall take you to Midgard, where you'll find the Village of Svara. The name Valkamor is known there. We warn you, though: as you discover your past, do not lose sight of what matters in the present."

Soon enough, the heroes came to another boulder. Brunhilde had left the dwarven site in a hurry, and Thundercluck needed a moment to catch up with her. He started to investigate the rock, but Brunhilde smacked it with her sword and shouted, "An open mind!"

Another tunnel appeared.

"This must go to Midgard," Brunhilde said. "And to Valkamor!"

Thundercluck remembered Odin's rules. The king had said, *Given your recent playtime in Midgard, you are not to use the Bifrost again until you have the book.* Thundercluck raised his brows and wondered, *Are we allowed to go there?*

"Relax," Brunhilde said. "Technically, Odin didn't say we can't go to Midgard *at all*; he just said we can't use the *Bifrost*. So let's go! But we can't take the Bifrost back to Asgard yet, if that's what you had in mind."

They entered the tunnel. Again they passed through darkness and rainbow crystals. "I wonder if Roy, Gee, and Biv dug this tunnel themselves," Brunhilde said.

They emerged on misty cliffs in Midgard. Ocean waves crashed against the rocks below. On the side of a distant mountain, a cluster of rooftops poked through the mist.

"That must be the Village of Svara," Brunhilde said. "I wonder if that'll lead us to Valkamor himself!" Now that they were out of Jotunheim, there were no more giants to fear. The heroes took flight.

A moment later, Medda crept out of the tunnel. She still held Gorman's skull. War-Tog followed and said, "Can I carry Mr. Boss again? I like bein' helpful."

"You still have a role in my plans, pig," Medda said. "Otherwise I'd have left you long ago."

"What now?" Gorman asked. "We've been sneak-
ing everywhere. It's a miracle War-Tog made it by the
dwarves without being seen."

"Hide-an'-seek is m'favorite game," War-Tog said.

"My point is," Gorman said, "if we follow those two
to the village, we'll have a hard time staying hidden."

"We're not going to the village," Medda answered.
"Let the children seek their precious Valkamor. As for
us, we have a big night ahead." She lifted Gorman's
skull to look him in the eye sockets. "We need to cook."

CHAPTER 10
VALKAMOR

THUNDERCLUCK AND BRUNHILDE LANDED
in the mist near the edge of the village. Brunhilde
patted Thundercluck's shoulder.

"After we beat Gorman," she said, "remember how
we came home and everyone called us heroes?"

Thundercluck nodded.

"Brace yourself for more fanfare," Brunhilde said.
"Everyone knows our story. No matter how happy these
Vikings are to see us, remember, we have to focus on
finding Valkamor."

They entered the village and saw a pair of Vikings

speaking loudly as they left a store called SHIELD SHACK.

One held up a wooden shield and said, "With this I'll be invincible, like Bruno Hildebrawn! They say he defeated Gorman Bones with his trusty sidekick, Thunder Eagle!"

Brunhilde leaned to Thundercluck and whispered, "Bruno Hildebrawn?"

Thundercluck's eyes went wide. *Eagle?* he thought. *And SIDEKICK?*

"Nonsense!" the other man said. "It was no eagle, but a thundering falcon!"

Thundercluck and Brunhilde exchanged annoyed glances. "Those two might not be the best people to ask," Brunhilde said. "But look!" She pointed to the store's wooden sign. Between the words "shield" and "shack," the letter "v" had been carved and scuffed over, as if someone had tried to erase it.

"Could that be for Valkamor?" Brunhilde asked. They entered the store.

The store was empty except for the shopkeeper. Brunhilde approached him and said, "Greetings! We've come in search of Valkamor. Where might we find him?"

The shopkeeper snorted. "The Monster Slayer?" he said. "Those are just stories, things we tell children to make them feel safe. Half this town seems to think the legends are true, but it's impossible. Nice wings, by the way...and what's a chicken doing in my shop?"

Brunhilde frowned. "Clearly, the chicken is shopping," she said. "Is there anyone else who might have information on Valkamor?" Under her breath, she added, "Maybe something actually helpful?"

"I'll speak no more of Valkamor," he said. "If you won't let it go, perhaps you'll like the Sword Master. He's right around the corner outside."

Brunhilde left the shop brimming with energy, and Thundercluck hurried to keep up. "Did you hear that?" she said. "Maybe my dad's a Midgardian Sword Master! I . . . don't know exactly what that is, but it sounds cool!"

Can we stop for a snack? Thundercluck wondered, but Brunhilde was on a mission.

When they rounded the corner, Brunhilde frowned. The "Sword Master" was a boy about her age sitting under an awning that said SWORD SHACK. Wooden training swords were spread across a table in front of him. He looked at Brunhilde and said, "Nice Valkyrie costume. Can I help you?"

"It's not ... ahem. We're looking for Valkamor," Brunhilde said.

"Oh, my dad must have sent you. I'm Osvald," said the boy. He tapped a wooden sword. "It's a family business. 'Buy a shield, then give it a whack at the Sword Shack!' That's what dad always says. We also sell gauntlets at the Glove Shack. It's a little ol—"

"That's nice," Brunhilde replied. "So about Valkamor ..."

"The Guardian?" asked Osvald. "Dad doesn't like to hear it, but I know what I saw!"

"You've seen him?" Brunhilde asked.

"Oh, I've seen a lot," the boy said smugly. "If you're so into this stuff, I'll tell you what I know." He tossed her a wooden sword and added, "But first, you have to spar with me."

Brunhilde caught the sword and said, "I don't think that's—"

"What's the matter," said Osvald. "You chicken?"

Thundercluck narrowed his eyes and thought, *That was uncalled for.*

Brunhilde gripped the wooden sword. "You're on."

Medda led War-Tog and Gorman to her hideout, an abandoned fortress rising in the mountains. The villains climbed a spire and looked out into the mist. The Village of Svara was barely visible in the distance.

War-Tog looked around the run-down tower. The man-pig brushed a cobweb off Gorman's skull and

said, "I like your tower, Miss Medda. With all these rats and spiders, you must never feel lonely."

Gorman was less impressed. "Some of us prefer to live with style," he said.

Medda scowled and said, "Even at the peak of your power, you were a sad little king on a sad little hill."

"It was a volcano, thank you very much," Gorman replied.

Medda rolled her eyes. "When you spend as much time as I have searching the realms for secrets, you find what shelter you can. And the only thing that concerns you here is this: we have a kitchen."

"Ooh, Boss," War-Tog said. "I'll bet you'll like that."

"I'm listening," said Gorman.

"I'll take you to the kitchen soon enough," Medda said. She glanced toward the village and asked, "Pig, do you still have my spyglass?"

"Oh, you mean the Nosy-Scope?" War-Tog said excitedly. He had been carrying it on his back, and he held it out for Medda.

She snatched it from his hands and said, "Let's check on our little friends."

Next to the Sword Shack, Brunhilde and Osvald stood face-to-face in a sparring area. A small crowd of Vikings gathered around. Brunhilde gave her shield to Thundercluck for safekeeping, and she exchanged her real sword for a wooden one from the shack's selection.

"The lender sword for your first match is free," Osvald said, picking up a training sword of his own. "Now, let me explain a few things about swords."

Brunhilde took a battle stance and said, "Thanks, but I've already—"

"No, see, you're doing it wrong," he said. "You're keeping your wrist flexible, but actually, you should grip the sword as tight as you can. Swordplay is all about who's got the stronger grip, so no flexibility in the wrist."

Brunhilde cocked an eyebrow and said, "That's . . . the opposite of—"

"Now, when you're using a sword," Osvald said, "it's important to do a lot of twirls and flips. A real swords-man does those all the time. The cooler you look, the better you are at swordplay."

Thundercluck tilted his head. *Even I know that's not right*, he thought, *and I'm a chicken.*

"You know what?" Brunhilde said. "I think the best

way for me to learn is through practice. You go ahead and attack. I'll try to defend, and after that . . . you can give all the advice you like."

Osvald made a smug face and answered, "If you say so."

He lunged at Brunhilde and swung his sword. In one fluid motion, Brunhilde dodged to the side, tripped him with her foot, and knocked the sword out of his hand. He tumbled to the ground, and the sword flipped through the air. Brunhilde caught it.

"Maybe I'm CATCHING ON," she said. The onlookers were silent. "Get it? Catching on? 'Cause I caught the sword. Come on, guys, that was—" Then Brunhilde went quiet as she spotted a hooded figure in the crowd.

People stood aside as the figure came forward. Someone whispered, "Valkamor!"

The newcomer raised a wooden sword to Brunhilde. The figure's face was hidden in the shadows of a cloak, but the gesture was clearly an invitation.

The feathers on Thundercluck's neck stood up. For a moment, he even forgot he was hungry.

Back in the Asgardian Throne Room, the ravens Huginn and Muninn flew to Odin's wrist. "Ca-caw!" they said, and Odin nodded intently.

"Terrible news indeed," he said. "Freya and the search party have found no trace of the children. Heimdall has gazed upon all the realms, and he cannot see them, either. What are we to do?"

Frigg, Thor, and Odin began speaking over one another. Frigg wanted Odin to change his rules. Thor wanted to join the search. Odin insisted his rules were final.

Saga sat quietly, but her head perked up as if an old friend had just appeared in her mind.

"What now, fortune-teller?" Odin said crossly. "Another rhyme about some secret you know and we don't?"

Saga said nothing in response, but a smile crept across her face.

Brunhilde sparred with the cloaked figure. They were a pair of whirling robes, their wooden swords clacking in speedy rhythm.

By Thor's hammer, Thundercluck thought, *I've never seen Brunhilde this well matched!* Out loud he whispered, "Bugahh."

The duelers pressed their swords together. They struggled for a moment and launched each other backward.

"Whoa!" Brunhilde said, her feet sliding through the dirt. She wiped her brow and whispered, "Who *are* you?"

The figure's hood fell back to reveal a woman's face. From within her cloak, she spread a pair of wings. She looked like Brunhilde, but older, and she had a scar on her cheek. Teardrops danced on her lashes.

"I've waited so long for this," she said. "My name is Sigrun Valkamor. Brunhilde ... I'm your mother."

PART III

THE SNACK ATTACK

CHAPTER 11
THE TREE HOUSE

THE WOODEN SWORD FELL FROM BRUN-
hilde's hand. She stood in shocked silence, then ran to
Sigrun. The two embraced.

Thundercluck watched and wondered, *Should I join
them, or give Brunhilde some space?*

Brunhilde caught his eye and said, "Come here,
buddy!" He joined the hug. "This is Thundercluck,"
Brunhilde said. "He's family, too."

"I know," Sigrun said with a smile. A tear ran
down the scar on her cheek, and she wiped it away.
"I've heard all about you two. I'm so proud." Before

Brunhilde could respond, Sigrun added, "We have much to discuss, but best do it away from listening ears." She stood back and held Brunhilde's hands in her own. They both bowed their heads and touched wing tips together.

Thundercluck tilted his head, puzzled. Brunhilde whispered, "That's a sacred gesture for a Valkyrie's trust. If a Valkyrie does it when she's lying, the feathers on her wings start smoking."

Thundercluck looked at his own wings and imagined smoke coming out. *I'd be a spicy chicken*, he thought.

Sigrun spread her wings. "Grab your things, and let's go home," she said. She took flight, and the heroes followed.

The villagers gave confused waves. As the trio flew away, they heard Osvald say, "I *told* you Valkamor was real!"

Up in the air, Brunhilde tugged on Sigrun's sleeve. "Did you see me spar with that Sword Master kid?"

"Yes," Sigrun said. "You did very well. Of course, you're Asgardian, so compared to him you have super-strength. But since he's the one who challenged you, he was literally asking for it."

"He said he knew about you," Brunhilde said. "What did he mean?"

Sigrun laughed. "One time I saved him from an aggressive goose," she said. "Since then, he's considered himself an expert on monster attacks and all things Valkamor."

Thundercluck's stomach grumbled as he soared. *I hope Sigrun's house has snacks,* he thought, *'cause all I've eaten today is half a bagel.*

"When the dwarves called me daughter of Valkamor," Brunhilde said, "I thought you were my dad."

Sigrun smiled and said, "I like the name Valkamor to be known, but I've aimed to keep an air of mystery about it. As for your father, well, that's a story for another time." She gave her wings a sharp flap.

"Was he a hero, too?" Brunhilde asked.

"He was a man of many secrets," Sigrun answered.

"We're not exactly on good terms. Speaking of secrets, did you find my journal?"

"Well," Brunhilde said, "Thundercluck and I checked it out from the library a while ago, but then we kinda lost it."

What do you mean, "we"? thought Thundercluck. *And what do you mean, "kinda"?*

Brunhilde went on, "Somehow the Book Wyrm took it."

Sigrun's eyes bulged. "By the gods! The Book Wyrm is . . . formidable."

"You've faced it?" Brunhilde asked.

"We're almost home," Sigrun said. "Let's discuss inside."

They descended from the sky to a forest. Sigrun waved her hand at a wide tree. A knot in the wood expanded, revealing a door on the trunk. "Welcome," Sigrun said, "to my tree house. It's enchanted so that only those a Valkamor invites may enter. Please, come in."

"Invitation only?" Gorman said, looking up from the Nosy-Scope. War-Tog was holding it to his skull at the tower's window. "I suppose you need something in that tree house."

"How perceptive of you," Medda said flatly, snatching the scope away. "And now you see why we need your recipe. Speaking of, how exactly will you cook?"

"I'll dictate," Gorman said, "and War-Tog will do the grunt work. And he really does grunt."

War-Tog nodded.

"What of your smoke magic?" Medda asked. "Teleportation spells?"

"Ooh, Boss used to love doing those!" War-Tog said. "He'd always say, 'Get out of my sight,' and warp me somewhere else, like he wuz sendin' me on a little vacation."

"My magic has been...somewhat compromised," Gorman grumbled, "but if I put my head to it, I can still cast a spell or two."

"Good," Medda said, peering again through the

spyglass at Sigrun's home. "That will prove most useful." With her back to War-Tog, she ordered, "Pig, take Gorman downstairs. The kitchen is on the left. It's just past the moldy couch—don't try to sit there; the roaches have claimed it. You find the oven, and I'll keep an eye on the children. We'll be visiting them soon."

Thundercluck beheld the tree house interior, which was far larger than the trunk had appeared from outside. Warm lanterns illuminated swords, spears, treasures, and maps. *But I don't see any snacks*, Thundercluck thought.

Brunhilde was a fountain overflowing with questions. Sigrun's answers came with a gentle smile.

"So you're a Valkyrie, too?"

"I was, just like you."

"What's your favorite weapon?"

"The sword, just like you."

"What kind of magic can you do?"

"Light, just like you."

Sigrun adjusted her sleeve, briefly revealing a bracelet on her wrist. It was shaped like a snake whose jaws
were firmly clenched on its own tail. Brunhilde looked
at her own bracelet. The snake's mouth hovered, ready
to bite. She asked in a quieter voice, "Mom ... were you
banished?"

Sigrun gestured to a table,
whose chairs scooted themselves back. "Have a seat,"
she said. "It's a long story."

CHAPTER 12
SIGRUN'S STORY

THUNDERCLUCK AND BRUNHILDE SAT down. Sigrun remained standing and looked at Brunhilde's wings. "Those were so tiny the day you were born," she said. "Not every Valkyrie is born with her wings, you know—entry to our Sisterhood can take many paths." She sat down and began her tale.

I was an orphan in the realm of Vanaland, just a child when Freya found me. Odin was wary, but Freya said she saw an

undeniable spark in me. *She knew what it meant to be an outsider—she herself had come to Asgard from Vanaland after the realms had made peace.*

She blessed me with the Ritual of the Wings, and suddenly I could fly. In Asgard I found a new world of magic and adventure. Best of all, the Valkyrie Sisterhood gave me a family.

Thundercluck remembered arriving in Asgard and feeling like he finally belonged. *I hope she can tell us where the book is, so we can find it and go home,* he thought. He hoped Brunhilde would ask Sigrun more about the Wyrm. He also hoped they would have dinner soon.

Brunhilde listened breathlessly to Sigrun's every word. Thundercluck decided not to interrupt. Sigrun went on:

My best friend was another young Valkyrie in training. We both wanted to become the greatest Valkyrie of all time. If I may be so bold, we were true contenders. My friend was better at fighting; I was better at flying. My friend was a perfect student; she always made the honor roll, and she volunteered as Hall Monitor of Valhalla. As for me, well, I had a bit of a rebellious streak.

Sigrun paused to look at Brunhilde's bracelet. She smiled and said, "That might run in the family, dear. I take it you're in trouble over my journal. Did the librarian mention that another book had been lost?"

Brunhilde remembered Madame Runa. "She said it only happened once before. Did you take the other book?"

"No," Sigrun said. "My friend did."

My friend was a shape-shifter. She had enormous potential, but she resented that her powers had limits.

She grew stronger with training, but it wasn't enough for her. She scoured the library for books about shape-shifting. All she found was a pamphlet called Your Changing Body, and that turned out to be something else entirely. Desperate, she turned to the library's restricted section.

My friend saw the library as a source of great power. I just liked that it was quiet. One night I was there, relaxing after a long day of training, and I heard a noise. It was my friend. She had flown to the top of the tallest bookshelf, and she stole a forbidden book.

She thought no one was watching, but she was wrong. I saw it.

The next day, Odin asked if I knew about the book. I didn't want my friend to get in trouble, so I lied. I pretended I knew nothing.

Then Odin asked my friend, and she lied, too. She said she knew the thief. She said it was me.

"I lied to help her," Sigrun said, "and she lied to hurt me. I had never felt so betrayed."

Thundercluck leaned his head against Brunhilde. She patted his neck feathers.

"It didn't matter what we said," Sigrun went on. "Madame Runa can sense when a book is taken, and Heimdall saw what happened from his watchtower. Odin knew we both lied. He banished us both."

"That's not fair!" Brunhilde said.

"Maybe not," Sigrun replied, "but I still had my wings and my magic."

Brunhilde glanced at her own bracelet and asked, "You get to keep all that after banishment?"

"Yes," Sigrun said, "but you can't go back to Asgard or contact any Asgardian, and no one there is allowed to search for you."

Uh-oh, Thundercluck thought. *We searched for Sigrun. I don't want to get in any more trouble!*

Sigrun caught his eye and said, "Don't worry. I

imagine Odin doesn't like telling my story, and if you didn't know I was banished, you weren't forbidden from finding me."

With a shaky voice, Brunhilde asked, "Is that why nobody told me about you?"

"For some, it was that," Sigrun said. "For Odin, it was pride."

Brunhilde looked again at her bracelet. "What was it like after you left?"

"I had many adventures," Sigrun said. "And my favorite of all was the day you were born."

Brunhilde went very quiet. She wiped her eye and whispered, "Then why didn't you want me?"

Sigrun leaned forward and gently kissed Brunhilde's forehead. "I assure you," she said, "nothing could be further from the truth."

After our banishment, things were never the same with my friend. We eventually went our separate ways. On my own, I traveled the realms and discovered all kinds of magic. I fell

in love, and I had you, my wonderful girl. We settled here in Midgard.

When you were almost a year old, I took you out for a stroll. You couldn't stand on your own yet, but if you held my hands and fluttered your wings, you could almost balance on your feet. It was a good day . . . until a monster attacked.

With you in one arm and my shield in the other, I could only fight back so much. And when I tried to flee, the monster was right on my heels. Then I saw a rainbow in the sky, and I was faced with a horrible choice: keep you in danger, or give you up to safety?

Seeing a rainbow meant Asgard was using the Bifrost. If a worthy soul reached the rainbow before it faded, it could take them to Asgard as well. Since I was banished, I couldn't use this escape myself, but I knew you could.

I flew to the rainbow. The monster gave chase. I hated to let you go, but the only thing worse would have been to keep you in harm's way. I held you into the beam, and you vanished.

Then my sword hand was free, and my heart was full of fury. I whirled around and unleashed a blinding arc of light. The monster recoiled and fled. I dropped to the ground. The rainbow was gone, and so were you.

"I've never cried so hard in all my life," Sigrun said. "I didn't know if I'd ever see you again, but I never gave up hope."

"Was there no way you could reach me?" Brunhilde asked.

"When you became Asgardian," Sigrun said, "my

banishment meant I couldn't contact you. I tried holding letters into a rainbow, but they wouldn't vanish—right in my hands, the words 'Message Not Sent' appeared on all the envelopes. But one night, I heard Saga's voice in a dream. She said I would see three more rainbows, and I could use them to send three gifts. I couldn't address them to you, but I hoped they'd reach you all the same."

Brunhilde raised her brows.

"The next time I saw a rainbow, I used it to send a message that simply said, 'Her name is Brunhilde.' The time after that, I sent my Battle Bag." Sigrun paused to add, "It looks nice on you, by the way. And finally, years later, I sent my journal in a chest."

Thundercluck remembered finding the chest in the library. They had opened it with a feather from Brunhilde's wing.

"Then I wandered the realms," Sigrun said. "I put my Valkyrie training to use and became a monster hunter."

"Did you ever find the one that attacked us?" Brunhilde asked.

Sigrun's gaze became distant. "No, that one's ... sneaky. It can take on many forms. But I did all I could to help people, and to spread the name Valkamor far and wide. I hoped that, if I couldn't find you, maybe one day you'd find me. And here you are."

In the fortress kitchen, Gorman's skull sat on a counter, directing War-Tog at the oven.

"Tell me, pig, does it have a setting for cooking with the all-consuming fires of Ragnarok?"

"Uhh ... I see RADIANT BAKE, Mr. Boss."

"Close enough."

Medda leaned in through the doorway and asked, "How goes it? And shouldn't you have a cookbook— your precious *Recipe Book of the Dead*?"

"Alas," Gorman said, "it was lost when Castle Igne-ous fell. But I can make this recipe from memory. We'll need ingredients, though. We have sugar, salt, and baking powder. We need behemoth butter, nightmare milk, and two cups of dark-purpose flour. Can you find all that?"

With a poof of smoke, Medda transformed to her horned owl form. "I can find anything," she said. "I'll be back before—"

She was interrupted by a long slurping sound. War-Tog had set Gorman's skull on the floor and started eating gruel from a bowl. He took  another long slurp, then looked at Medda and said, "What?"

She returned to her normal form and glared at him. "I can't concentrate when you slurp like that," she said. "Where did you get ... *whatever* that is, and more importantly, are you almost done with it?"

"Oh no, ma'am," War-Tog said. "This is a magical bottomless bowl Boss gave me. It always has more gruel if I want it, and since we don't hafta be sneaky right now, I thought I'd have a snack." He took another long slurp and smacked his lips.

Medda gave him an icy look. "Did you know *The Recipe Book of the Dead* contained powerful secrets?"

War-Tog nodded.

"When Castle Igneous fell, did you ever think to grab the cookbook instead of your precious gruel bowl?"

War-Tog shook his head.

"You disgust me," Medda said. "Stay here and wait for further instructions."

War-Tog hunched his head and returned to his gruel, muttering the words, "Not very friendly."

"So once you're banished," Brunhilde said, "there's absolutely, definitely no way back?"

Sigrun looked into the distance and said, "I found one glimmer of hope on my travels. There's a three-word spell Odin can say to undo the banishment."

"Really? Great!" Brunhilde said. "What's the spell?"

"That's the thing," Sigrun replied. "It's three specific

words, but no one knows what they are. It's an ancient form of magic where even the spell caster cannot be told the words, but must say them from the heart." Brunhilde was quiet, and Sigrun added, "Knowing Odin, I wouldn't hold my breath."

Thundercluck shifted awkwardly in his seat, thinking, *I just want everyone to get along. And I want to find the book—I want to go home!* His stomach growled again, and he thought, *Also, I want a snack.*

"Clearly," Sigrun said, "I don't see eye to eye with Odin. But he did give you a home, and he did keep you safe."

"Yeah," Brunhilde said, "right up until he let the kingdom fall under a curse, and I had to go save it."

Thundercluck tilted his head and thought, *You mean, WE had to save it, right?*

"You know what?" Brunhilde said. "If Odin doesn't want you in Asgard, he probably doesn't want me there, either. Maybe I won't go back!"

Thundercluck's eyes went wide. He said a worried "Bagaww?"

Brunhilde looked at her bracelet. "This doesn't exactly make me feel valued, you know. Let's stay here for the night, and we'll see how we feel in the morning."

The chicken's eyes widened. This would be their second night away from Asgard, meaning tomorrow was the deadline to find the book! He gave an impatient "Braawk!"

Brunhilde whirled on him and said, "You don't know what it's like! I worked my wings off all my life to be a hero—I trained twice as hard as everyone else, and no one seems to appreciate it. You just sat on a farm a few years, and suddenly greatness happened for you."

Thundercluck's beak fell open. His first reaction was to think, *That's not my fault*, but he also realized, *She's not wrong.*

"I'm going for a walk," Brunhilde huffed. She got up and stomped out the door.

Thundercluck sat in shocked silence. Sigrun patted him and said, "I'll talk to her," then walked out the door as well.

The sun had begun to set, and the forest was getting dark. Brunhilde sat under a tree with her arms crossed. Sigrun joined her.

"You've been treated unfairly," Sigrun said, "and you have a right to be angry. But do you think Thundercluck is the enemy?"

Brunhilde sighed and said, "No. I should talk to him." She hugged her mom and went back to the tree house. The trunk's door was still cracked, and Brunhilde peeked inside.

"Hey, Thundercluck," she said. "I wasn't thinking before. No matter how we got here, we're in this

together, and what matters most is we lift each other up. I . . . Thundercluck?"

She looked around the tree house interior, but Thundercluck was nowhere to be seen.

CHAPTER 13
STORMING OUT

IN THE WOODS OUTSIDE, THUNDERCLUCK

stomped as hard as a chicken could stomp. His neck pumped with each step. *Greatness just happened to me?* He shook his head. *I didn't have it easy. I never belonged on the farm. I didn't just waltz through our last quest—I was so scared of Gorman! Who overcame all that, and who saved the day? Me!*

Moonlight shone through the dark trees, and Thundercluck remembered how lost he would have been without Brunhilde's help. *I'm not mad,* he tried to tell himself. *She's my friend.* Then his stomach growled.

But all she brought to eat was that nasty sourdough! And her mom—what kind of host invites people in without offering a snack? And ALL I'VE EATEN TODAY IS HALF A BAGEL!

He saw a horned beetle and remembered he was no longer in Jotunheim. Now he was in Midgard, where worms and bugs were edible again.

The beetle wiggled its horns. Thundercluck sprinted toward it with his beak wide open.

The beetle darted away, and Thundercluck crashed into some bars. He tripped over a wire, and something clicked shut behind him. He was in a birdcage. With a poof of black smoke, the beetle transformed into a woman and said, "Got you!"

Thundercluck pointed his wings at her. His feathers began to spark.

"Don't try to shock me," she said.

He tried to shock her. His bolt flowed through the cage bars and into his own feet. "BWAAK!" he squawked, and smoke rose from his feathers.

"Typical," the woman said. "This cage was crafted to hold magical beasts. Stay quiet." He squawked again, and the woman tied a ribbon around his beak. He tried to break through it, but to his surprise, it held firm. "Woven by the dwarves," the woman said, "and taken while they weren't looking. You'll be working for me now."

"He's over here!" Brunhilde's voice rang out. She and

Sigrun came running into view. They stopped a few paces from the birdcage.

"Medda!" Sigrun yelled. "You let that chicken go!"

"You . . . know her?" Brunhilde asked.

Thundercluck struggled against the ribbon on his

beak, and Medda picked up the cage. "Hello, Sigrun," she said. From under her crimson cloak, she unfurled a pair of wings. "Long time no see."

Sigrun drew her sword. "Brunhilde, remember my best friend I told you about? Well, here she is."

Brunhilde thought back to the story and asked, "Didn't you say you wished her well?"

"That was then," Sigrun answered. "Remember how I said a monster attacked us, one that could take on

many forms?" She pointed her sword at Medda. "It was her."

By the majestic mustache of Thor! Thundercluck thought. He tried to cluck, but with his beak tied shut, all that came out was "Mrrm-blrrk."

"Ah, memories," Medda said. "That scar on your cheek has healed nicely. It suits you." She pulled a jar from her sleeve and waved it at Sigrun. It was full of thorny green vines and leaves. "Your journal will be mine," she said, "and so will vengeance. Now, War-Tog!"

War-Tog stepped out from behind a tree, holding Gorman's skull.

"Good evening," Gorman said, "and goodbye!" His jaw opened wide, and two huge clouds of smoke burst out. When they cleared, the forest was empty.

All six of them—Gorman, War-Tog, Medda, Sigrun, Brunhilde, and Thundercluck—had vanished.

CHAPTER 14

THE MIDNIGHT SNACK OF SHADOWS

BRUNHILDE AND SIGRUN COUGHED AS the smoke around them cleared. Rock walls surrounded them on three sides, and beyond the light of a single torch, a cave extended into darkness. Brunhilde still had her bag, but all their weapons were gone. A large cot sat beside them.

"Where are we?" Brunhilde asked. She looked around. "And where's Thundercluck?"

"One thing at a time," Sigrun said. She pinched some dirt from the floor and felt it between her fingers. "We're still in Midgard." She sniffed the air and added, "But something smells like Jotunheim."

A familiar chatter echoed through the cave. Red lights glowed in the darkness. The smell of hot peppers drifted through the air. Brunhilde groaned and said, "Aw, not these guys again."

The Fire Ants of Jotunheim crept into view. Some carried torches in their mandibles. They had the Valkyries cornered.

"What's going on?" Brunhilde asked. The ants continued to chatter, and Sigrun listened intently. Brunhilde's eyes widened, and she asked, "Do you know their language?"

"Bits and pieces," Sigrun replied. "It seems they were expecting us. These ants are sentries—they're not here to fight us, but they won't let us leave. We're being held until court with their grand leader at dawn." She leaned to Brunhilde's ear and whispered, "That might be our time to escape. For now, we should rest if we can."

They sat on the cot together. Brunhilde's head spun thinking about the day's events. She turned to Sigrun and asked, "What does Medda want?"

"Revenge," Sigrun replied. "When she and I were banished, I moved on. She didn't. She hated that I found happiness, so she made me suffer. Now if she gets my book, she'll make *everyone* suffer."

"Why does she want the book?" Brunhilde asked.

"She wants to poison the well," Sigrun said.

"You mean...figuratively, she wants to bad-mouth—"

"Literally," Sigrun said, "there's a magical Well of Eternity, and Medda wants to poison it."

High aboveground, another cloud of smoke cleared. War-Tog, Gorman, Medda, and the caged Thundercluck stood in Medda's tower.

From War-Tog's hands, Gorman's skull gazed at Thundercluck. "Hello, chicken," he said.

Thundercluck rattled his cage and tried to squawk. The ribbon on his beak held firm.

"Easy, now!" Gorman said. "For once I'm not trying to eat you. Quite the opposite: I want to feed you."

Thundercluck became still. He was suspicious but very hungry.

"That's a good chicken," Gorman said. "Now, Medda, shall we show our new recruit what we've made?"

From the sleeve of her crimson cloak, Medda pulled out a biscuit on a string. Thundercluck froze, transfixed. The mouthwatering treat even had gourmet birdseed sprinkled on top.

Medda swung the string back and forth, and Thundercluck's eyes followed. He had seen friends fall victim to enchanted snacks before, and now he tried to resist the biscuit. *The world is full of good biscuits*, he thought, *but don't trust that one!* But that voice in his head seemed to shrink as his hunger grew. Medda grinned and spoke the words:

> *By secrets in the darkest mist,*
> *By humor in the gallows,*
> *No hungry hero can resist . . .*
> *The Midnight Snack of Shadows!*

Thundercluck's pupils became slits. All his repressed anger came back. His stomach let out a low growl, as if his belly felt as mad at the world as he did.

"It's working," Gorman whispered. Then he said aloud to Thundercluck, "Would you like that biscuit?"

The voice in Thundercluck's head had become muffled. He nodded.

Medda swung the biscuit closer and asked, "Would you do *anything* for it?"

He nodded again.

War-Tog cleared his throat. "Um, Boss," he said, "I don't wanna be too critical, Mr. Boss, and maybe

I don't understand right, but ... I think maybe wut we're doin' isn't very nice."

Gorman chuckled and said, "Oh, War-Tog."

With her free hand, Medda snatched Gorman's skull from War-Tog's hands. "If you don't like it, pig," she said, "you can leave. We don't need you anymore. As a matter of fact, I'll help you pack!" She grabbed the bottomless gruel bowl and threw it out the door to the stairs. It clattered down the steps, growing quieter the farther it fell away.

War-Tog looked to Gorman, but the cook's eyes were fixed on Thundercluck. War-Tog slumped and slowly left the tower.

"The Well of Eternity?" Brunhilde asked. "Thundercluck and I tried to go there back when we had your book."

"I know," Sigrun said. "You were captured by Gorman, but Thundercluck saw it."

"How do you know all this?" Brunhilde asked.

"The well is home to Urd, an ancient being who sees all," Sigrun said. "I met her on my own travels, and we have ways of keeping in touch. The well is a place of great power, and if the wrong person finds it, they could wreak havoc on the realms."

"We were trying to reach a rune-stone that would take us there," Brunhilde said. "Couldn't anyone just use that stone all the time?"

"It's not so simple," Sigrun said. "The path to the well is ever changing—if you went back and looked for that same stone where it was before, it wouldn't be there now. Urd enchanted my journal so it could always find the well. If Medda gets that book, we're in trouble."

"What would Medda do?" Brunhilde asked.

"The well is connected to the roots of all existence," Sigrun said. "If poison is dropped into its waters, the effects will flow through all the realms. Did you see what was in Medda's bottle?"

Brunhilde remembered a glimpse of thorny vines and leaves. She realized she had seen them before. "The Poison Ivy of Alfheim," she whispered.

"Yes," Sigrun said grimly. "The Vine of Eternal Itch."

"Freya said its touch would itch for ages," Brunhilde said, "and extreme exposure is deadly."

Sigrun nodded. "If Medda gets to the well, she'll inflict that poison ivy on everyone. There will be no escaping her wrath . . . her itchy, itchy wrath."

Medda dangled the biscuit closer to Thundercluck. His mouth watered.

"Good biiird," Medda sang. She set Gorman's skull on a counter and untied the ribbon from Thundercluck's beak. "Just eat the biscuit, and you'll be ours to command . . . against your pesky little friends."

A spike of willpower rose up in Thundercluck, and he turned his beak away. The biscuit's aroma lingered, still tempting him.

"Impressive," Gorman said.

Medda's voice went flat. "Can we just force-feed it?"

"No," Gorman said. "The spell only works if it's his choice."

"Fine." Medda broke the biscuit into halves and lightened her voice again. "Sweet little chicken, how about this? Just eat half the biscuit now, and we'll talk about the other half later." She wiggled one half by the cage bars.

Thundercluck's resolve weakened. He nodded. He gobbled it down.

Momentary relief and joy flowed from his belly to his feather tips. Then came the bad thoughts.

I shouldn't have eaten that . . . but it's Brunhilde's fault. She only cares about herself. She doesn't care about me.

He shook his head. *That's the evil biscuit talking! I don't want the other half.* He licked a tasty crumb off his beak. *Or do I?*

Medda stepped back to Gorman. "Did it work?"

"He was supposed to eat the whole thing," Gorman replied.

"Let's test it, then," Medda said. "Thundercluck!"

The chicken snapped to attention.

"Reach your wings through the bars of the cage."

Without meaning to, Thunder-cluck followed her command.

"Put your right wing in."

He obeyed.

"Put your right wing out."

He obeyed again.

"Put your right wing in. And now, shake it all about."

I must escape this hocus-pocus! Thundercluck thought. *I've got to turn myself around!* But he felt powerless to resist.

"Excellent," Medda said.

"Part of him is still trying to fight back," Gorman warned. "He needs to finish the snack."

"Oh, this?" Medda said, flashing the remaining biscuit half. "He'll give in eventually—I can see it in his eyes. But first he'll have to earn it." She leaned forward. "You see, chicken..."

She opened the cage, and Thundercluck's eyes widened. *A chance to fight back—a chance to escape!* But all he could do was sit still.

Medda grinned and whispered, "You're working for us now."

CHAPTER 15
DIFFERENT BEASTS

ALL NIGHT BRUNHILDE'S MIND SWIRLED
with worry, but eventually she slept. She woke to Sigrun shaking her shoulder. The cave was still dark, but Sigrun whispered, "It's dawn."

The sentry ants marched them through the twisting tunnel, descending lower into the cave.

As they marched, Sigrun whispered, "Be ready in case there's a chance to escape. Follow my lead."

Finally the cave widened into a large dome lined with torches. At its center, an especially massive ant sat on a throne of glowing coals. The ant wore a tiny crown.

"The Royal Court of the Colony," Sigrun said. "Brunhilde, we should bow. That's the queen."

Brunhilde bowed but stayed alert, ready to leap into action if the right moment struck.

The queen began to chatter. The sound echoed through the chamber, and Sigrun closed her eyes to focus. "The time for Royal Breakfast draws near," Sigrun said, "and . . . she demands . . . the bread?"

Brunhilde jolted upright and remembered her snack pouch. She pulled out what was left of the sourdough and asked, "This?"

The queen's chattering intensified. A pair of sentry ants came into the chamber pulling a cart that held the Valkyries' weapons.

"That's what she wants," Sigrun answered. "She says her scouts gave her crumbs they found in Jotunheim. She wants more. If you give her the loaf, she'll return our weapons and set us free."

"But it's *sour*dough," Brunhilde said. "I thought ants liked sweets."

The queen saw Brunhilde's confusion and chattered again. Sigrun translated: "She says she likes all kinds of carbohydrates, sourdough included."

"Same," Brunhilde said. "But I know a chicken who hates the stuff. Different yeasts for different beasts, I suppose." She thought a moment and said, "I'll give the bread, on one condition: her ants have to stop interrupting picnics."

Sigrun made a chattering sound and tapped her knuckles as if they were mandibles.

The queen nodded her head.

Sigrun turned to Brunhilde and said, "It's a deal."

With their weapons returned, Brunhilde and Sigrun emerged from the ant colony. They arose from a hole in a big pile of dirt.

"So we're done here," Brunhilde said, brushing the dirt off her hands. "That was easy!"

"Too easy," Sigrun replied. "Medda is capable of far worse treachery than that. I fear this was only a distraction. Hold out your sword."

Brunhilde drew the Dwarven Blade, looking around for enemies. Sigrun touched the sword's hilt and said:

> *Oh Dwarven Blade, oh sword*
> *of gnome,*
> *Now guide this Battle Maiden*
> *home.*

The sword began pulling in Brunhilde's hand.

"My forest is close," Sigrun said. "The tree house is your home now as much as mine. The sword will guide you. Wait for me there—I need to consult with some old friends."

Brunhilde flew back to the tree house, worrying the whole way about Thundercluck. When she arrived, though, she found him waiting by the tree. He appeared to be unharmed. If anything, he looked bored.

"Buddy! You're all right!" she said. "How did you escape?"

The chicken did not respond.

"You must not have gotten much sleep," Brunhilde said. "Your eyes look all weird. Anyway, we're supposed to wait here." She waved her hand like she remembered her mother doing, and the door reappeared on the trunk.

Brunhilde entered, but Thundercluck waited outside, staring at her impatiently. "Oh, right, the enchantment," she said. "I have to invite you—uh, please come in."

Thundercluck waddled right past Brunhilde without looking at her. Then he started rummaging through Sigrun's treasure chests.

"Thundercluck, what are you doing?" Brunhilde said. Again he ignored her. He opened cupboard after cupboard, then unbuckled a treasure chest and jumped in. Brunhilde could only see his tail feathers. She stepped closer and asked, "Are you hiding?"

His head popped up with a golden envelope. Holding it in his beak, he hopped out of the chest and started toward the door.

"Thundercluck, stop!" Brunhilde said, positioning herself between the bird and the doorway. "Talk to me!" she said. "Or at least cluck!"

Thundercluck tried to run past her, but she put her hand on his chest. Brunhilde glared and said, "You're being a jerk, chicken!"

Still holding the envelope in his beak, he dug his claws into the tree house floor. He pushed against Brunhilde's hand. Without thinking, she whopped him with her shield.

Thundercluck stumbled back and scowled at Brunhilde. "What's gotten into you?" she demanded. He
crouched low and pointed his wing tips in her direc-
tion. It was the stance he took to launch a lightning
bolt.

"Whoa, wait," Brunhilde said. "Whatever's going on,
don't shock me! I can't use my magic."

Thundercluck lowered his wings, and for a moment
Brunhilde thought he had been joking. Then he glared
at her and gave his wings a flap. A gust of wind blasted
out. It blew Brunhilde through the doorway, and she
landed outside on her back. Thundercluck flew past, the
envelope still in his beak. By the time Brunhilde got
back on her feet, Thundercluck was gone.

Moments later, Sigrun returned.
She looked at Brunhilde's face and
asked, "What happened?"

"Thundercluck stole something,"
Brunhilde said. "He's ... something's really wrong."

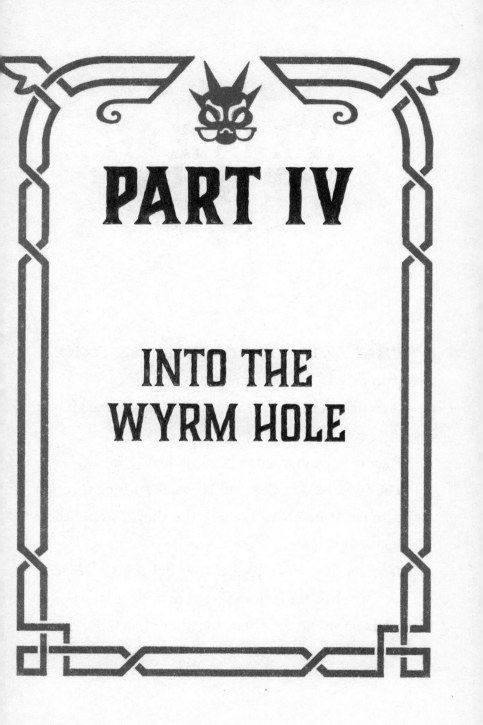

PART IV

INTO THE
WYRM HOLE

CHAPTER 16
THE TALE OF THE WYRM

"WHAT DID THUNDERCLUCK TAKE?" Sigrun asked.

"I couldn't tell," Brunhilde said. "It was some kind of golden envelope."

Sigrun's gaze hardened. "This is bad," she said.

The dwarves Roy, Gee, and Biv came rushing through the forest. When they saw Sigrun, they lowered their helmets in respect.

"For the last time, please stop doing that," Sigrun said. "Brunhilde, I believe you've met my friends?"

"Valkamor and daughter, together at last," Roy said.

"I owe you some thanks for that," Sigrun replied, "but we need to talk. The card has been stolen."

The dwarves' tunics remained as vibrant as ever, but the color drained from their faces.

"What's the card?" Brunhilde asked.

"Everyone, please come inside," Sigrun said. "It's time Brunhilde learns the truth about the Book Wyrm."

Inside the tree house, Brunhilde sat facing Roy, Gee, and Biv over the table. Sigrun dug through chests and curios, muttering, "Where is it? I swear, as soon we save the universe, I'm having an ancient-relic yard sale."

Roy leaned forward and asked, "Daughter of Valkamor, what do you know of the Book Wyrm?"

"Uh...you can just call me Brunhilde," she said. "And let's see: Wyrms are super rare, and super powerful, with invincible scales and razor tails and acid spit. And the Book Wyrm likes to read. Sound about right?"

"All true," Roy said, "but there is more to the story than you know."

Sigrun said, "A-*ha*!" and joined them, holding a wide saucer and a jar of water. "This water is from the Well of Eternity," she said. "It's a sacred gift from Urd herself." She poured the water into the dish and set it on the table.

Images flickered in the air over the water. Brunhilde saw moments from her own past—games she'd played with Thundercluck, and her Valkyrie training—as well as Sigrun and the dwarves in various realms.

"When it's far from its source," Sigrun said, "the well's water acts as a memory prism, making the past visible. Unheld, it won't focus on anything in particular. But, Roy, if you'll hold the saucer . . ."

Roy closed his eyes, lowered his head, and held the saucer with both hands. The images over the water calmed.

". . . then we can show Brunhilde what she needs to see."

Above the saucer, Brunhilde saw a mirage of Roy

entering a cave. Gee and Biv followed, carrying a huge pair of spectacles.

"Your beards look shorter there," Brunhilde said.

Across the table, Gee replied, "Yes. What you see happened centuries ago. Short beards were in fashion back then."

"Wyrms are sacred creatures in Nidavellir," Biv added. "We found one in a cave and crafted those spectacles for it—they granted the Wyrm the power to read."

"You created the Book Wyrm?" Brunhilde asked.

"We did," Roy said, his head still bowed and his eyes still closed. "We hoped it would allow dwarves and Wyrms to communicate. We were wrong." The mirage lingered on the cave's dark entrance, and the sound of a roar echoed through it. "Over the centuries, many memories have dulled," Roy said, "but I'll never forget that roar."

"Indeed," said Gee. "Once the Wyrm could read, it had no interest in talking. It just wanted more books. We only brought one, and its title was *You're First Book* . . . with the wrong spelling of 'your.' The Book Wyrm was enraged."

Biv shivered.

The mirage shifted to a door slamming in a tunnel. A bonfire burned in front of it, and a line of dwarves approached, each tossing an envelope into the fire.

"A tragic day," Gee said. "The Book Wyrm took over Nidavellir's underground library, and our king decreed we lock it shut forever. He even ordered all Dwarven Library Cards be destroyed, so no one could enter the library's doors."

"So much knowledge lost to the ages," Biv said. "For a time, we thought it was worth it—at least the Wyrm was contained. But its magic was greater than we realized. Outside the library, books began to vanish."

The saucer's mirage shifted. Scene after scene showed dwarves looking for missing books. They checked bags, counters, and coffee tables, then shrugged and scratched their heads.

Without looking up, Roy said, "The Book Wyrm had conjured a spell: anytime someone forgot about an overdue library book, it would vanish into the Wyrm's collection. To this day, many think their books are simply misplaced. But make no mistake: powerful magic is at play."

Brunhilde recalled forgetting about the Valkamor book and how it had seemed to vanish. "Oh," she said.

"As the library continued pulling in books," Gee added, "its old purpose was forgotten, and it came to be known by a new name."

Biv nodded and whispered, "The Wyrm Hole."

"The vanishings began in Nidavellir," Roy said, "but soon they spread throughout the realms. By creating such a monster, we brought shame upon the Dwarven Kingdom. We were cast into exile for our deeds."

The mirage showed Roy, Gee, and Biv skulking away from a mass of angry dwarves. Roy let go of the saucer, and the memory faded.

"We've been tunneling through the realms ever since," he said, "hoping to find a warrior who could defeat the Wyrm."

"You were exiled?" Brunhilde said. "That means banished, right? Does *everyone* just ignore their problems and banish people?"

Sigrun cleared her throat and said, "Some rulers have convinced themselves that's leadership."

"So if that's where the book is," Brunhilde said, "how do we get there?"

"Dwarven mages sealed the Wyrm Hole," Roy said, "but we can help you get close. Of course, entry is only possible with a Dwarven Library Card."

"And those were all destroyed?" Brunhilde asked.

"All but one," the dwarf replied. "When we left, we smuggled out the last card in existence."

"We entrusted it to Valkamor," Gee said, nodding at Sigrun, "but—"

"That's what Thundercluck stole, isn't it?" Brunhilde asked.

"It is," Sigrun said. "Medda's behind this, and if she has the card, she's going to the Wyrm Hole. We have to stop her ... which means we may have to face Thundercluck again."

Thundercluck arrived at Medda's tower with the Dwarven Library Card. He perched at the window and lowered his head. *What have I done?* he thought. *I feel so guilty, I've almost lost my appetite.* His stomach gurgled, and he thought again, *Almost.*

Medda snatched the card. She waved the remaining biscuit half and asked, "Hungry, little bird? Too bad!" She tucked the biscuit back in her sleeve. "We're not done with you yet—get back in your cage."

Involuntarily, Thundercluck returned to the cage. Medda slammed it shut, then turned to Gorman and asked, "Ready to teleport again?"

Gorman had an ice pack on his forehead and dark circles under his eye sockets. "I have a head-ache," he groaned, "and since I don't have a body, that means all of me is aching right now."

"Oh, don't be so dramatic," Medda scoffed.

"Do you know how hard it is

to warp six different people to points A and B, and two sets of weapons to point C?" he snapped. "It's arcane magic and a math exam all at once." Medda glared at him. He looked around at the cramped tower and softly added, "It'd be easier in an open space."

"Fine," Medda said, lifting him in her hand. "I'll take you outside, and you'll take me to the Wyrm Hole. Thundercluck, too."

Thundercluck squawked. Medda whipped around and said, "Are you mad at us for bewitching you, bird? Well, I have a secret: it only worked because you already resented your friend. We didn't make you betray her; we just gave you a little nudge. And how did I know it would

work? Because if you spend enough time with someone, sooner or later you end up hating their guts.
That's the true nature of friendship."

"If Thundercluck's turned bad," Brunhilde asked, "is it
wrong for me to fight him?"

"It's one thing to support a friend who's struggling,"
Sigrun said, "but you don't owe someone loyalty if
what they're doing is wrong. Whatever choice you
make, I'm on your side."

"How can we face him?" Brunhilde asked. She looked
at her bracelet. "I'm not supposed to use my magic.
Should I just break that rule? If I get banished from
Asgard . . . Mom, can I live with you?"

Sigrun lifted Brunhilde's chin and held eye contact
with her. "I would love that. But if you leave Asgard,
I want it to be because that's your *best* choice, not
because it's your *only* choice. Maybe there's a way we
can do this without using your magic."

"How?" Brunhilde asked.

"I don't know," Sigrun said, "but I have a friend who might. Look into the saucer."

Brunhilde peered at the water from the Well of Eternity. Though only she and Sigrun leaned over the saucer, another woman's reflection looked back at them.

"Greetings, Battle Maiden," said the woman. "I am Urd, the Watcher in the Well. We must talk about your friend."

CHAPTER 17
A WORD WITH URD

BRUNHILDE STARED AT URD'S REFLECTION
in wonder. Sigrun put a hand on her shoulder.

"We mustn't stay long," she said. "Roy, Gee, Biv, and

I are going outside to prepare for our departure. Take this moment to discuss with Urd."

Sigrun and the dwarves left the tree house. Brunhilde was alone with the saucer. She looked at Urd and asked, "So how do you know Mom?"

"She found my well on her travels," Urd said. "The Dwarven Blade you wield—did you know it once belonged to her? She entrusted it to me, in case you found my well before you found each other."

"And Thundercluck brought it to me," Brunhilde said. "We got along so well then. What's happened to him?"

"He has been bewitched," Urd replied, "by the Midnight Snack of Shadows."

"I bet I know who cooked it," Brunhilde said flatly.

"It is a recipe that can take many forms," Urd said. "It corrupts the mind of the one it infects. Thundercluck has tried to resist it, but the spell is feeding upon his anger."

"What could make him mad enough to turn on me?" Brunhilde asked. "I'm his best friend!"

Urd's gaze was steady. "Sometimes those closest to us can make us feel the worst," she said, "even if they don't realize it. If you wish to stop Medda, you have two options: break the spell on Thundercluck, or defeat him in battle."

"Without my magic, how could I do either one?" Brunhilde asked.

"If you choose the path of battle," Urd said, "you will learn more of what your Dwarven Blade can do. Even without your own magic, the blade can absorb others' power and cast it back at them."

"Maybe a taste of his own medicine is just what he needs," Brunhilde muttered. She took a deep breath and said, "But he's still my friend. If I just want to break the spell, do you have some kind of magic relic for that? Like, a 'Chill Pill for the Chosen,' or—"

"It is not an object you need," Urd replied. "The counterspell is an ancient form of magic, one that even the most powerful beings find difficult. A two-word incantation can break the curse, but you must discover those words on your own."

Brunhilde thought a moment.

"Does 'doo-doo head' count as two words, or is that three?" she asked.

"Keep searching," Urd said. "The words must be spoken from the heart."

Medda carried Gorman and Thundercluck out of her tower. Thundercluck swung back and forth in his cage, still feeling guilty, hungry, and mad at the world.

"Here we are, bonehead," Medda said, stopping at an open area. "Any more excuses, or are you ready to teleport?"

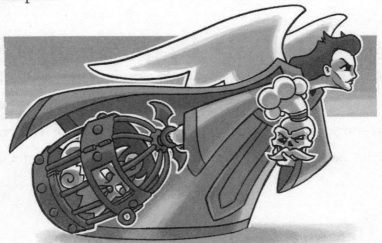

"It'll make my headache worse, but so does your pestering," Gorman replied. "We might as well go." He glanced at the large footprints from War-Tog's exit the night before. "I never imagined I'd miss that pig, but at least he was polite."

"Boo-hoo," Medda said. "Now let's go already." She lifted Thundercluck's cage and added, "Don't forget the chicken!"

"I know." Gorman sighed. "I'll bring the whole crew."

"So," Brunhilde said, "I've got to either beat my best friend in a fight, or use a specific spell to break the curse on him, and I can't be told what it is. Anything else I should know?"

"Yes," Urd said, "one final warning. Thundercluck has only eaten half of the Midnight Snack of Shadows—if he eats the other half, the curse will be complete. The coming confrontation may be your last chance to turn him back. If you do not break the spell, and instead choose an all-out-fight . . . no matter who wins, your friendship may forever be broken."

Brunhilde frowned.

"Anger has come between you both," Urd said. "You can use your words or use the sword. The choice is yours."

The tree house door opened, and Sigrun leaned inside. "We're ready," she said. "It's time."

CHAPTER 18
THE HEROES' DUEL

WITH A PUFF OF SMOKE, MEDDA, GOR- man, and Thundercluck arrived in Nidavellir, standing before a corridor of pillars engraved with ancient symbols. Years of neglect had left the carvings cracked and covered in moss. The pillars led to a hole in the side of the mountain.

"The Wyrm Hole," Medda said. "Locked away for centuries! Only a few know of your secrets, and fewer still have entered. But lucky me," she said, pulling the envelope from her robe, "I have a card up my sleeve!"

She set down Thundercluck's cage and held Gorman's skull to her eye level. "Hide yourself where you can still see the hole," she said, "and wait for me to emerge! Then we'll talk about your bones." She leaned closer and whispered, "And your chicken."

Gorman wheezed and disappeared in a poof of smoke.

"Now, bird," Medda said, "do as I say, and perhaps you'll be rewarded." She flashed the remaining biscuit half from her sleeve.

Thundercluck tried to shake his head, but instead he nodded.

Medda pointed to the Wyrm Hole. "Within that tunnel, there's a locked door. After I go in, it'll remain open for one hour. You wait here at the entrance, and if those Valkyrie fools come snooping, don't let them past."

Thundercluck cocked his head and thought, *But I'm in a cage.*

"Oh, they'll let you out," Medda said. "The cage unlocks easily from the outside, and your little friend is a sap! Just like her mother. When they set you free, that's when you attack."

She placed the cage at the tunnel's entrance and walked in.

Thundercluck felt hungrier than ever, and tired, too. *Brunhilde was right*, he thought. *I didn't sleep well last night.* His heart skipped a beat. Two nights away from Asgard meant today was the deadline to return the book.

I wish we weren't in this mess, he thought. *I wish Brun-hilde and I could just get along again.* Then their last encounter came back to him. *But who does she think she is, saying I looked weird? That's rude. I'm not tired at all. I'm fine! I can stay awake!*

Without another thought, he fell asleep.

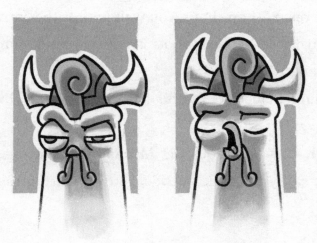

Brunhilde followed Sigrun out of the tree house. Roy, Gee, and Biv waited outside. Roy held a wooden case. He opened it to reveal a key just like the one on Freya's necklace.

Brunhilde raised her brows and asked, "Is that a Spectrum Key?"

"Indeed," said Roy. "A crowning achievement of dwarven crafting, though only a truly powerful magic user can wield it." He handed the key to Sigrun.

"I've been summoning energy for it all morning." She turned to Brunhilde. "Due to their exile, Roy, Gee, and Biv cannot follow. You and I are going to the Wyrm Hole alone."

Roy handed her the key and bowed his head. "May the fates smile on your journey," he said. He looked at Brunhilde and added solemnly, "May your chicken not go bad."

Sigrun closed her eyes and whispered:

Unlock a door between the realms,
with light in magic waves:
Nidavellir, Nidavellir, the land of dwarven caves!

She turned the key in midair, and a portal opened before them. While Freya's portal had been large enough for a whole chariot, Sigrun kept hers small, and Brunhilde ducked to step through. Sigrun leaned forward and followed.

They stood at the Wyrm Hole's entrance. At the tunnel's edge, they spotted Thundercluck sleeping in his cage.

Sigrun turned the key again, and the portal thinned to a sliver. "I must use all my energy to keep it open," she said. "If it closes, we're stranded—I won't have the power to open another. I'm afraid you'll have to face Thundercluck alone."

Brunhilde nodded and took a step toward the

cage. Thundercluck's eyes fluttered open, and he hopped up from his nap.

Brunhilde tried to think of two words to break the curse. "Hey, buddy," she said.

He looked mad.

"You okay?"

He still looked mad.

"Calm down."

Now he looked even madder.

"Hmm," Brunhilde said. "Maybe if I let you out of that cage, we can figure this out." She was wary of getting too close, so she used her sword to lift the cage's latch.

"BAWAAK!" Thundercluck burst out and started pecking. Brunhilde blocked with her shield, then waved it to thrust Thundercluck away.

He skidded back through the dirt, then dashed at Brunhilde again. Sparks danced on his feather tips—a sign that lightning was building up within. Brunhilde kept dodging and blocking.

She tried to think of more two-word phrases. "Stop that!" she yelled between parries. "Bad chicken!"

The feather sparks intensified. He dug his talons into the ground.

"Uh . . . please don't?" Brunhilde said. For a moment

she wondered if those could be the words, but Thundercluck looked madder than ever.

He pointed his wings, ready to launch a bolt.

"If that's how it's got to be," Brunhilde said, "then FINE!" She swung her sword. As the blade came near, Thundercluck struck it with lightning.

The contact pushed Brunhilde backward, but she held firm, remembering Urd's advice about the Dwarven Blade. When using her own magic, Brunhilde had always

imagined pushing light outward through the sword. Now she did the opposite and imagined pulling inward. The sword began to glow blue as it absorbed the lightning.

The charged blade felt foreign in her hand. She slashed, and an arc of lightning hit Thundercluck. He hurled into one of the pillars, which split at the base with a loud CRACK!

Thundercluck fell to the ground.

"Serves you right," Brunhilde muttered, but immediately regretted it. She had not meant to think those words, much less say them aloud.

Thundercluck scrambled to his feet. He looked more angry than hurt. He dug his feet in and pointed his wings again.

He launched another bolt, but Brunhilde was ready—she drew it into her blade easily. She hesitated, not wanting to strike Thundercluck again. The sword trembled in her hand, like it might burst unless she attacked.

She slashed to the side, this time shooting lightning

at the pillar Thundercluck had hit. The crack in its base grew. The pillar started tilting.

Thundercluck was charging up another bolt, gathering more power than before. Brunhilde wondered if too many strikes might break the sword—if so, she needed to win the fight first. She needed to attack.

Then the teetering pillar caught her eye.

It began to fall, and Thundercluck stood directly in its path. Without thinking, Brunhilde ran to him, held up her shield, and cast out a magic dome of protective light. The pillar collided with the light, bursting into rubble that fell at their sides.

Thundercluck paused to look at Brunhilde, bolt still at the ready. Brunhilde had dropped her sword and wrapped an arm around him. Her shield magic glowed around them. The snake on her bracelet bit its own tail.

Thundercluck and Brunhilde both stared at the bracelet, then at each other.

"Guess I'm banished now," Brunhilde said. She smiled and added, "Worth it."

The dome of light faded.

"We've been hurting each other," Brunhilde said. "Even before we were fighting, I know I said some mean things." The two-word incantation came to her, and she said the words aloud just as Thundercluck thought them:

"I'm sorry."

Medda and Gorman's curse was broken. All of Thundercluck's anger was replaced by sorrow. Tears welled up in his eyes. He leaned his head on Brunhilde's shoulder and thought, *I've been a rotten chicken.*

"No matter who started it," Brunhilde said, "what matters is we're past it. You're still my best friend. Truce?"

Thundercluck nodded with a gentle "Bagaw."

"And hey, I brought you something," Brunhilde said, pulling a bun from her bag's snack pouch. "It's no biscuit, but it was the best I could find in Mom's pantry."

Thundercluck gobbled it down. He was still hungry, but he felt more peaceful than he had before.

Sigrun came up behind them. Still concentrating

on her tiny portal, she rested her free hand on Brun-hilde's helmet and said, "I'm proud of you. Not every friendship comes back from that kind of fight. But if you kids can do it, who knows? Maybe there's hope for the rest of us." She looked at Medda's footprints going into the Wyrm Hole.

Thundercluck frowned. *That door would only stay open an hour,* he thought. *How long has it been?* He darted into the tunnel and tried the door within. It was locked.

Guilt welled up like ice water in his chest. Brun-hilde and Sigrun joined him. "Most who know this place think this door is the only way in," Sigrun said. "But we still have one hope. Follow me."

She led them around a bend in the cliffs to a boulder on the mountainside. "We need to move that rock," she said. "Normally I'd push it myself, but I must focus on the key. So, kids, if you please . . ."

Thundercluck and Brunhilde pushed the boulder. With their combined might, they moved it to the side. *Good to be a team again,* Thundercluck thought.

The surface behind the boulder had a tiny square

hatch. Sigrun inhaled and said, "The Ancient Dwarven Book Return. It's too small for me or Brunhilde . . . but just the right size for a chicken."

Thundercluck gulped.

"Last time I was here," Sigrun said, "I used that boulder to seal it away."

"Last time?" Brunhilde asked. "You've been here before?"

"Yes," Sigrun said. "Years ago, I saved Roy, Gee, and Biv on one of their adventures. They gave me the Dwarven Library Card, and they asked if I could defeat the Book Wyrm. I tried. I failed. Of all the monsters I've faced, that was the first time I'd had to retreat."

"What about Medda?" Brunhilde asked.

"Medda is devious indeed," Sigrun said. "But as I said, her powers have limits—there are three. First: she can only take the form of creatures with horns. Second: she can only take a creature's form if she's touched it with her hand. And third: staying in a creature's form takes great concentration, especially if it's a new one. But even with these limits, she is a force to be reckoned with."

Thundercluck tried to gulp again, but his throat felt stuck. *I'm up against a devious shape-shifter and an unstoppable serpent*, he thought. *And the serpent's well-read.*

Brunhilde saw his worried eyes. "I believe in you," she said. "Remember, if you get the book, you can go back to Asgard, and maybe Odin can unbanish me and Mom. But if Medda gets the book, everyone in the universe gets deadly poison ivy."

Thundercluck tilted his head.

"It's a long story; just trust me," Brunhilde said.

Thundercluck nodded. He took a deep breath and fluttered to the hatch.

The chicken entered the Wyrm Hole.

CHAPTER 19
A WYRM WELCOME

THUNDERCLUCK TIPTOED THROUGH THE
Dwarven Library, a network of darkened chambers
and caves. He saw hundreds of bookshelves half-
empty and candles unlit, all forgotten for centuries.
With tiny zaps, Thundercluck lit
the candles.

In their warm glow, he saw
countless books had been knocked
to the floor; more still were piled
in corners and hallways. To Thundercluck's dismay, it seemed the

Wyrm had been wrecking the books. Some had been punctured, some had been sliced, and others still had been burned. Thundercluck remembered the Wyrm had a razor tail and acid spit.

I hope the Valkamor book is all right, Thundercluck thought. *And if the Book Wyrm likes to read, why would it damage all these books?* Then he heard a rhythmic hissing sound.

HISS ... pause ... HISS ... pause ... HISS ...

Thundercluck crept toward the sound. He zapped another candle, and something glimmered ahead. The candle's light reflected off of sharp, shiny scales. The Book Wyrm lay before Thundercluck, fast asleep.

Thundercluck fluttered onto a bookshelf and looked at the Wyrm in awe. The serpent was enormous, with scales and horns that shimmered like crystals. A pair of glasses rested on its angular head. Its body was curled in a spiral, coiled around the Valkamor book.

A wave of relief washed over Thundercluck. The book was intact, the Wyrm was asleep, and the chicken saw no sign of Medda. *Well, well, well*, he thought, *the early bird gets the Wyrm.* He was about to flutter over and quietly grab the book, but a screech rang out in the air.

The Book Wyrm's eyes snapped open as a horned owl entered the chamber. *Medda!* thought Thundercluck. The owl screeched again and swooped for the book. The Wyrm sprang into motion, slashing with its tail, but Medda dodged. She soared at the Wyrm's face, and with a poof of smoke, she transformed to a lamb in midair.

The Wyrm stared at the lamb, too confused to react. Medda landed on its nose, shouting, "Lamb . . . CHOP!" She struck the Wyrm's forehead with a hoof. The

Wyrm flinched, and Medda was enveloped in another poof of smoke.

For a moment Thundercluck lost sight of her. *Can she teleport, too?* he wondered, but then he spotted a tiny horned lizard. It ran along the Wyrm's scales, heading straight for the Valkamor book.

Oh no you don't! Thundercluck thought, and he launched a bolt at the lizard.

Medda jumped aside. The bolt bounced off of the Wyrm. The serpent lunged, and Medda shifted to a horned toad, hopping from shelf to shelf. Thundercluck could barely keep track of her.

Watching the toad, the Wyrm opened its jaws to launch an acid spray. It burned the base of a bookshelf just as Medda landed on it, and the shelf collapsed. A poof of smoke came from beneath it, and a ram burst out of the shelf's remains.

The Wyrm charged at the ram, and the two locked horns. The enormous Wyrm started pushing Medda toward a corner. Medda transformed from ram, to bison, to rhinoceros, but still the Wyrm was mightier. Concerned, Medda returned to her normal form.

The Book Wyrm towered over her. "Nice serpent," she said, patting its scales with her hand.

Thundercluck saw the Valkamor book had slid away from the action. *While those two keep each other busy,* he thought, *I'll just take the book and skedaddle.* Then he recalled the rules of Medda's powers, and his eyes went wide.

She can take the forms of creatures with horns, he thought, *but only if she's touched them with her hand.*

A huge cloud of smoke erupted, and a new Wyrm reared up with a bone-chilling cackle. The Book Wyrm recoiled, and Medda-Wyrm attacked.

Brunhilde peered into the Dwarven Book Return. Sigrun held the Spectrum Key and whispered incantations. Brunhilde took a deep breath and said, "I hope Thundercluck's all right in there."

Medda's nefarious laugh echoed out through the hatch.

Medda and the Book Wyrm lashed and bit at each other. Their struggle knocked over bookshelves and sent fountains of acid sailing through the air. Thundercluck ducked under a bulky wooden desk and thought, *Boy, isn't this a can of Wyrms?*

The Valkamor book was just out of reach. *If I make a run for it,* Thundercluck thought, *one of the Wyrms might get me. I have to stop Medda, and she can only keep that form if she's concentrating. Maybe I can break her focus!*

He looked out from under the desk. Both Wyrms were a blur of shiny scales. *Which one's Medda?* Thundercluck wondered, but he could barely make out the Book Wyrm's glasses.

Have at you! Thundercluck thought, and he cried, "Bagock!"

He launched a lightning bolt at Medda's Wyrm form, but the magic just bounced off her scales. The flash blinded the Book Wyrm for a moment, and Medda took the chance to strike. She slithered around the Book Wyrm and squeezed.

Thundercluck tried to shock her with an even bigger bolt, but again it had no effect. His energy was getting low, and his hope sank even lower.

Then he heard a long *sluuuuuuuurp*.

"WHAT WAS THAT?" Medda said, her Wyrm voice amplified and terrible.

Another slurp echoed in the chamber, followed by a snort.

"I TOLD YOU I CAN'T CONCENTRATE WHEN YOU DO THAT!" Medda shouted.

War-Tog walked out from behind a bookshelf with his bottomless bowl of gruel. He held steady, deliberate eye contact with Medda. He slurped more gruel and smacked his lips.

Medda started twitching. "HOW DID YOU GET HERE?" she demanded.

"I snuck in after you, while Mr. Thundercluck wuz sleepin'," War-Tog said. He took another slurp.

Medda's hold on the Book Wyrm weakened. "No," she said, her voice still distraught, but less forceful than before. "I meant, how did you get to this realm?

You left my tower, and I didn't tell Gorman to bring you here!"

"I didn't go far, and I wuz mindin' my own business," War-Tog said. "Suddenly there wuz smoke swirlin' around me. Mr. Boss musta warped me here, too. I think he really cares about me." He smacked his lips again and let out a long burp.

Medda shuddered and said, "Of all the moronic things you've said, that has got to be the most preposterous!"

"And yet," War-Tog replied, "here I am."

The Book Wyrm broke free of Medda's grasp and retreated to a shadowy corner of the room. Medda cried out in fury as she collapsed into her normal form. She looked at Thundercluck and whipped out the Midnight Snack of Shadows.

"You, bird!" she said. "Still hungry? Shock that pig away, and this can at last be yours!"

Thundercluck's stomach growled. His eyes locked on the biscuit. He summoned another bolt, took aim, and released the thunder.

It blasted the Midnight Snack of Shadows out of

Medda's hand, and the biscuit burst into sizzling crumbs. Medda's sleeve caught fire. She flapped it out, shifted to her owl form, and fled the chamber.

All was quiet for a moment, and then War-Tog said, "Welp, I'd better go before I forget where the door is." He ambled away.

Thundercluck was left alone with the Book Wyrm. Barely visible in the shadows, the serpent narrowed its eyes.

Waiting at the book return, Brunhilde and Sigrun heard doors slamming open from the Wyrm Hole around the bend. They saw a horned owl soaring off in the sky.

"Medda," Sigrun whispered.

"She's getting away!" Brunhilde said.

"Let her go," Sigrun replied. "When Thundercluck comes out, we need to be here for him. Medda didn't have the book. It's down to Thundercluck and the Wyrm."

Brunhilde peered into the hatch and tried not to worry.

Thundercluck stared at the Wyrm. The Wyrm stared back.

What's my move? the chicken thought. *The Wyrm's just looking at me. Should I strike first?* He remembered his confrontation with Brunhilde. *I don't want to start another fight*, he thought. *From now on, I only want to use my power for self-defense or to help someone in need.*

He glanced at the Valkamor book, and so did the Wyrm. Behind the magic glasses, its expression was doleful.

Why isn't it attacking, Thundercluck thought, *and why is it sad?* He looked again at all the damaged books, and an idea occurred to him.

He waddled to a book that was still intact, careful to hold eye contact with the Wyrm. He opened the book with a foot, sat down, and used a wing to flip to the first page. Then he raised a brow at the Wyrm, hoping it would understand his invitation.

The Wyrm hesitated, then inched closer. Thundercluck angled the book for the Wyrm to see, and the creature came closer still. It settled behind Thundercluck, looking over the bird's shoulder.

Thundercluck had guessed the true curse of the Book Wyrm: it wanted only to read, but without any limbs, it couldn't turn pages. Every time it tried to use its horns, tail, or tongue, it could only destroy the books. Alone and unable to talk, it had no way to ask for help.

They began to read together.

Every time the Wyrm nodded, Thundercluck turned a page. The Wyrm was a fast reader, and before long the book was done. The serpent looked at Thundercluck, gratitude shining in its eyes.

Thundercluck pointed at the Valkamor book. The Wyrm seemed to understand, and it nodded.

Thundercluck thought about how often he felt ignored or misunderstood. "Bagurr," he said gently. He pressed his forehead against the Wyrm's nose and silently promised to return. Then he gripped the Valkamor book with his feet, gave a final nod to the Book Wyrm, and flew back to his friends.

Thundercluck emerged from the Dwarven Book Return.

"Hey, buddy! You did it!" Brunhilde exclaimed.

"Well done, bird," Sigrun said. "Now back to the portal, quickly!"

They returned to Midgard, and Sigrun closed the portal. She dropped the key like a heavy weight.

"Gee! Biv!" said Roy. "The heroes have returned!"

"We were victorious," Sigrun said, "but not without cost."

Brunhilde held up her bracelet for the dwarves to see. The snake's teeth remained clamped on its tail. "You've got the book," she told Thundercluck, "which means you can use the Bifrost. But I'm banished, so I can't."

She patted the chicken's neck, and he thought, *I don't want to leave you again.*

"We'll be right here," Sigrun said. "You're not allowed to search for us, but it doesn't count as 'searching' if you already know where we are."

"See if you can get Odin to change his mind," Brunhilde said.

"That may be your greatest challenge yet," Sigrun added. "Godspeed, good bird."

Thundercluck nodded. Remembering his Bifrost training, he held up a wing and thought of Asgard. The Valkyries stood back, and the chicken vanished in a beam of rainbow light.

CHAPTER 20
OVERDUE

THE DOOR TO ASGARD'S THRONE ROOM
burst open, and Thundercluck stormed in with the
book.

"The warrior bird returns!" Odin said. "But this is
not protocol. You should have taken the book to the
library, and waited for—"

Thundercluck slammed the book at his feet and said,
"Bwuk!"

"Well," Odin said, "what matters is you returned
the book before time ran out. Just barely, mind you.
And 'tis a shame about Brunhilde. We sensed when

she used her magic. That was against the rules. Her banishment is absolute."

"BWA-A-AAK," Thundercluck squawked. He fluttered his wings and added, "Bwok-bukbuk-BWAAK, bok bok!"

Odin stared at him blankly, then turned to Frigg, Thor, and Saga. He started to ask, "Do any of you understa . . ." but they all crossed their arms and shook their heads.

"Bu-gah!" Thundercluck said. He tried to act out everything that had happened since leaving Freya. He batted his lashes like a lamb, scuttled like a fire ant, snored like a giant, and spread his wings like Sigrun.

Then he cowered as if in a cage and pretended to scheme like Medda and Gorman. He performed both sides of his fight with Brunhilde. Finally he squirmed like a Wyrm, then he pecked at the book and repeated, "Bu-GAH!"

Odin stared in confusion. His two ravens perched on his shoulder. He whispered to them, "Do either of you speak chicken?" They shook their heads.

"Ahem," Queen Frigg said. "Brunhilde's the one who understands Thundercluck best. If she were here, perhaps she could interpret, but *someone* banished her from the kingdom for all of eternity."

Odin scowled and lowered his bushy white brows. "I already told you," he said, "my magic law is final. There's no way to undo it."

"Bukka-BWAAH!" Thundercluck said. He leapt and grabbed Odin's spear with his feet, then flew out of the Throne Room.

"Guards! Stop that bird!" Odin cried, but Thundercluck was already gone. Queen Frigg cleared her throat again. "Fine," Odin said. "I'll follow him."

Back at the tree house, Brunhilde held her bracelet to Sigrun's. She forced a smile and said, "We match."

A rainbow glowed before them, and a booming voice said, "You give that back!"

Thundercluck and Odin appeared, and with a flash the rainbow was gone. Thundercluck dropped Odin's spear on the ground and waddled to Brunhilde's side. He stood up straight and said, "Bugah."

Odin picked up his spear and stammered, "Why, Valkamor, is that you? And hello, Brunhilde. How do you do?"

"We've been busy," Sigrun said flatly. "Brunhilde just helped save the universe from terrible suffering... again. Is banishment the thanks she gets?"

"I... well," Odin said, "perhaps it would be nice to have her back in Asgard—both of you, really—but my magic cannot be undone. It's simply not possible."

"All sorts of things are possible," Sigrun said. "Urd

told me you can undo our banishment, but only if you say three magic words."

Odin paused, taken aback by Sigrun's boldness. "Well, I'm not saying I'll do it, but can you at least tell me what I'd have to say?"

Brunhilde jumped in to explain. "We can't. They must be discovered by the speaker and spoken from the heart."

"Three words," Odin repeated. "I shall give it a try." He counted on his fingers and declared, "I'll . . . allow . . . it!"

Nothing happened.

Odin counted again and said, "I . . . am . . . merciful!"

Again, there was no effect.

"Alas," he said, "I am out of ideas."

Brunhilde had been quiet, but now she blurted out, "You're giving up? I didn't give up on Thundercluck!" She held Odin's gaze and said, "I'm thirteen and a half.

You're literally thousands of years old. Why am I the mature one here?"

Odin went silent, and he realized what words he had to say. He grimaced like he was about to have a tooth pulled, and whispered, "... I was wrong."

The snake bracelets vanished from Brunhilde's and Sigrun's wrists.

"I was too harsh with both of you," Odin said. "I should have spoken with you more, rather than casting you out. I hope you'll come home to Asgard—can you forgive me?"

Thundercluck's heart beat faster. He had wanted so much to lift Brunhilde's banishment, it had not occurred to him she might not want to come back.

Brunhilde held Sigrun's hand and said, "I don't want to leave Asgard behind, but I want to be where you are, too. What do you say, Mom?"

Sigrun hugged her and said, "I spent over a dozen

years wishing we were together; I'm not about to part with you now." Then she looked at Odin. "Forgiveness takes time," she said, "but if you're willing to rebuild what's been damaged, so am I." She reached out her hand, and Odin held it in his own.

The elder god nodded at Thundercluck and said, "Quite a meeting you've brought me to! Well done, warrior bird."

Thundercluck fluttered to Brunhilde's shoulder. He raised his brows and said, "Buk-buk-bwah?"

Odin took a deep breath. "Young Valkyrie," he said, "I haven't given you enough credit. Asgard owes you its gratitude, and we welcome you home."

Brunhilde patted Thundercluck's neck. The chicken raised his wing. He, Brunhilde, Sigrun, and Odin vanished together in a beam of colorful light.

Asgard celebrated the adventurers' return with a feast in Valhalla. Brunhilde interpreted Thundercluck's story of the Wyrm Hole, and the kingdom was delighted.

Odin watched from a distance. His habit at ceremonies was to stand and speak, but it was dawning on him that he would do well to listen.

Saga came to his side. The goddess raised her staff and said:

Against another evil threat, our kingdom nearly failed.
Our heroes' bond was tested, but their friendship
still prevailed!
When facing foes nefarious, and blows unfairly struck,
We have ourselves a feathered friend . . .
in mighty Thundercluck!

EPILOGUE

WEEKS LATER, THUNDERCLUCK AND
Brunhilde returned to Nidavellir on an Asgardian
field trip. The realms had begun talking to each other
again.

The card remained lost, but the Dwarven Kingdom
found the library's door propped open with a gruel bowl.
The library of Nidavellir was accessible once more. Roy,
Gee, and Biv were welcomed home, and they invited the
Asgardians to a reading day with the Book Wyrm.

Freya led the trip, adamant that none of her students
would wander off this time. The librarian Madame